"You don't think it was an animal?"

Womack shook his head. "Any animal that could have torn those men up like that would have done so for a reason. It would have tried to make a meal out of those two or dragged 'em off somewhere to save for later."

"Could be the horses and cart scared it away," Slocum offered.

"Could be, but I've done some hunting and have found it takes a bit more than riding down a road to frighten anything other than a rabbit or deer. Something as vicious as whatever tore up those two would have stood its ground or stayed to protect its kill."

"A man, then. I don't know if that's better or worse."

"Whatever the hell it was, it don't get to tear apart two of my men and live to see another sunrise."

JAKE LOGAN

SLOCUM
AND THE BEAST
OF FALL PASS

JOVE BOOKS, NEW YORK

THE BERKLEY PUBLISHING GROUP
Published by the Penguin Group
Penguin Group (USA) LLC
375 Hudson Street, New York, New York 10014

USA • Canada • UK • Ireland • Australia • New Zealand • India • South Africa • China

penguin.com

A Penguin Random House Company

SLOCUM AND THE BEAST OF FALL PASS

A Jove Book / published by arrangement with the author

For information, address: The Berkley Publishing Group,
a division of Penguin Group (USA) LLC,
375 Hudson Street, New York, New York 10014.

ISBN: 978-0-515-15437-5

PUBLISHING HISTORY
Jove mass-market edition / February 2014

PRINTED IN THE UNITED STATES OF AMERICA

10 9 8 7 6 5 4 3 2

Cover illustration by Sergio Giovine.

1

Bennsonn was a town with only a few small things in its favor. One of those things, and easily the biggest, was the lumber mill around which the entire town had been built. It provided the steadiest stream of jobs and funds for the town while also bringing business into the entire county. Another element in Bennsonn's favor was its tranquil nature upheld by two different lawmen, who each had a few deputies working beneath him. It may have been a lot of law for such a small place in Oregon, but the mill was a valuable enough asset to warrant that kind of protection.

While Bennsonn had three saloons and the rowdies who were drawn to such places, the lawmen kept them in line. The trees surrounding the town on three sides were thicker than fleas on a stray dog's hide and never seemed to thin out no matter how many were chopped down and dragged across the mill's spinning saw blades. Most folks who lived there kept to themselves, helped their neighbors without much of a fuss, lent a hand wherever it was needed, and were in bed by a reasonable hour. Even the collection of three saloons that made up the town's entertainment district did a fairly good job of making sure any revelry didn't spill too far out into the street.

Eliza Yates normally liked the town's fragrant air and silent nights. At least, she did when she'd first arrived. After settling in and working at a tanner's shop for almost a year, she got an itch that she couldn't scratch. The discomfort ran deeper than her skin and made her feel like a dog gnawing at the rope that was keeping it from running free. For her, Bennsonn had stopped being quiet and had gotten boring. Since she didn't have the means to pack her things and find somewhere else to live, she did the next best thing and forged a new life right there in town.

As it turned out, all she needed to do was visit the town's saloons looking for work. She wasn't interested in doing the sort of work saloon owners normally wanted from a young woman with Eliza's pretty face and generous curves. After a bit of sweet talk to one establishment's owner, however, she landed a spot dealing faro.

The Second Saloon had one floor with drinking and gambling as well as a second floor that rented rooms to anyone looking for a place to sleep or to men indulging in what was provided by the women who did more than just deal cards to customers. Working there for most of her days and nights gave Eliza a different outlook on many things. She met folks other than the ones who rode into town to buy dry goods or trade the furs they'd collected from the woods and mountains scattered throughout Oregon's wilder lands. Even if she crossed paths with some of the same trappers and locals as before, Eliza now saw them in a different light as they kicked up their heels and gave in to their baser desires. The change was exactly what she'd needed.

Not all the men who found Bennsonn did so in search of tranquility or a job at the mill. Some of the strangers passing through carried guns on their hips and knew how to put those weapons to use. Eliza found those men a little frightening at first but very intriguing. She got plenty of chances to speak to them since those fellows were also the ones who brought money to gambling tables. They took risks and didn't abide with anyone taking anything from them. Eliza had even seen a few fights after working at the Second Saloon for less than a week. She liked the fights, although she would never admit as much out loud.

After eight months dealing faro, Eliza was no longer a stranger to the new life she'd chosen. She was recognized by most everyone who came in for a drink and didn't flinch when she had to stand up to a randy drunk or a man who figured losing enough money at her table entitled him to put his hands on her. Folks were used to seeing her there, which meant many of the men confided in Eliza even more than when spilling their guts to Rolf the bartender. One such man had come to town two weeks ago, but had been working at one of the logging camps outside Bennsonn for a while longer than that. He was tall and rugged and wore his Colt as if it was a vital part of his body. When he stepped through the front door now, Eliza couldn't help wondering about other parts of the man's body.

The only other player at her table when the rugged stranger came in for his most recent visit was an old man who'd lost the last two hands. As the old-timer turned his pockets inside out looking for more money to put on his favorite number, Eliza met the rugged man's eyes as he approached the bar. Another thing she'd learned about herself after a short time at the saloon was that she had no trouble holding a man's attention.

Eliza had thick, shoulder-length black hair, which formed a smooth slope ending at the base of her neck. Her face was slightly rounded, and when she smiled, it lit up like a pale moon. Her skin, smooth and white as cream, was displayed nicely by dresses that were cut low enough to show her ample bosom. She couldn't help brushing a few wisps of hair behind one ear when the rugged man across the room took notice of her. He grinned back at her before turning to face Rolf and order his drink. Eliza looked back at the old man at her table, knowing full well that the other one would be back sooner rather than later.

"What have you got for me, Dan?" she asked.

The old man shook his head while pulling a folding knife

and watch from one pocket. "Don't suppose I can bet with these?" he slurred in a voice that stank of stale beer.

"Sure you don't have anything else?" she asked. "Rolf doesn't like it when I try to guess how much something like that is worth."

"I can tell you how much it's worth."

"Why don't you try your other pocket first?"

Dan patted himself down and shook his head some more.

"Try your boot," Eliza said. "The left one."

Muttering under his breath, Dan bent down to pull up the cuff of his jeans so he could remove his boot. He overturned it and seemed more surprised than her when three silver dollars fell out to rattle upon the floor. "Well, I'll be damned!" he said. "You know me better than I know m'self!"

"Of course I do," she said with a smile. "I like to know my favorite players inside and out."

The truth of the matter was that she didn't know Dan any better than she did her other regulars. What she did know was that many of the men who stepped up to buck the tiger at faro weren't professional gamblers. They were mostly locals who wanted a bit of excitement to go along with their liquor, and those were also the types who kept money in their boots. For some strange reason, it was more often the left boot. There was no telling why that was, so Eliza had chalked it up to one of life's little mysteries.

"All right, then," Dan said while slapping one of his dollars on the seven. "Let's win enough to fill my other boot!"

"I'll do my best." Eliza dealt the hand without paying full attention. Her hands went through the motions and she only looked down at the spread to know what news to deliver. "Sorry about that," she said while putting on an appropriate frown. "Your luck's bound to change, though."

"Damn right it is," Dan said while placing another dollar on the same number. "Run it again!"

"You sure about that?"

"Far as I'm concerned, this here was found money. Found money is lucky money in my book. Run it again!"

"Here we go."

At the bar, the rugged stranger was finishing the beer he'd ordered and was leaning with both elbows on the bar. Eliza admired him from behind and smirked to herself as she dealt the cards. As if feeling the intensity in her gaze, the man turned around to look in her direction and tipped his hat to her.

"That's more like it!" Dan exclaimed.

Eliza looked down to see what she'd dealt and then looked again. "Sorry, hon," she said while tapping the cards. "You lost."

"I did?" Dan squinted down at the table and belched out a breath that was foul enough to make the entire table smell like spilled beer and sour milk. "So I did. Guess it's been a long night. One more time."

"Why don't you take some of that found money back home and save it for next time?" she asked.

"Ain't no need to save it, darlin'," Dan replied while eagerly placing the same bet he'd already lost twice before. "Every day should be lived like it was yer last."

Even though she was fairly certain Dan's wife wouldn't agree with that statement, she asked, "Run it again?"

"Run it again!"

She ran it again, taking her time since the rugged stranger was now making his way across the room toward her table. It didn't take much to deal a hand of faro. Even so, she felt as if a few minutes passed as she tried to recall whatever she knew about the handsome man. He was a poker player and known to drink more than his share of whiskey on occasion. He'd also given a few of the girls in other saloons a tumble between the sheets. She'd heard some stories from one of her friends who worked across the street at the Axe Handle, a competing saloon that provided more women than card tables. What she'd heard in that regard only made her more eager to make the rugged man's acquaintance.

"Hot damn!" Dan hollered. He squinted down at the table as Eliza shifted her focus back to where it belonged. After getting a second look at the cards that had been dealt, he slapped the table and said, "*Hot damn!* I really did win it this time!"

"You sure did. Here's your fortune." Eliza handed over the bit of money he'd won with a smile that grew even wider when she saw the rugged man standing directly in front of her and slightly behind Dan.

The man she'd been studying all this time was now studying her. He stood with a glass of whiskey in one hand and the bottle in the other. His Colt was strapped around his waist in a worn and battered holster. Before she could say anything to him, Dan pounded out an excited rhythm on the table and said, "Run it again! Run it again!"

Taking one breath was enough for the rugged man to catch a whiff of the stench billowing from Dan's drunken mouth. He scowled and turned to look at what was happening at the poker tables.

"You really should be going home," Eliza said.

"Why's that?" Dan grunted. "Ain't my money good here?"

"Of course it is."

Taking a turn toward the melancholy as drunks were known to do, Dan sighed, "Then maybe you're sick o' lookin' at me?"

Reaching out to pat his hand, Eliza said, "You know that's not true."

Someone had stomped into the saloon a moment ago, but Eliza had been too distracted to see who it was. There was no mistaking the voice now coming from the front part of the room, however. Dan's wife may have been a petite woman, but she was anything but frail.

"I'll just bet she ain't sick of you, you damn fool!" the short woman hollered. Dan's wife was less than ninety pounds soaking wet and had long silver hair tied behind her head so tightly that her face seemed to be made from stretched parchment. She walked like a man triple her size as she stomped toward the faro table.

Since Dan cowered when she approached, it was almost laughable when he said, "I can do what I please, woman!"

The old woman grabbed her husband's ear and pulled it as if she meant to tear it off his head. "You can do whatever you want so long as it's at home and you don't spend any more of our hard-earned money!"

"I found this money!"

"Then you should've brought it to me before coming here and handing it over to some saloon girl!" Glancing over to Eliza, she added, "No offense meant."

"None taken," Eliza said.

"But if you lay a hand on my husband, I'll cut it off."

The smile Eliza wore remained in place as she nodded and said, "Fair enough. I just deal cards around here."

"Keep it that way, missy. As for you," the old woman said to Dan, "you won't be comin' into town for a month if I have my say!"

Dan tried putting up a fight, if only to save face with his friends at the saloon. His efforts weren't very successful since he was attempting them while being dragged toward the door by a woman nearly half his size.

Everyone in the place watched the show for as long as it lasted. Once Dan and his wife were out of sight and the door was shut behind them, drinking resumed and cards were dealt.

"That was quite a spectacle," the rugged man said as he approached the table.

Eliza breathed easier, relieved that the old woman hadn't frightened him away. "It sure was," she replied. "No need for a stage when those two are around."

"Can I buy you a drink?"

"No need," she said. "I get my drinks for free. One of the benefits of working here."

The man was even handsomer when he laughed. "That's right. You must think I'm pretty stupid to say something like that."

"Not at all!"

He stood at the spot where Dan had been and looked at the layout in front of him. He then looked up at Eliza and winked. "I'm not normally a man to play this game. Odds are tipped too far in the house's favor."

"What sort of games do you like?" she asked.

"Poker. Among other things."

Eliza licked her upper lip and flushed when she realized what she'd done. Although she was no innocent when it came to entertaining men, she wasn't anything close to brazen. "I haven't played much poker," she said. "But I can deal some faro for you if you like. Maybe the odds will be in your favor this time."

The man reached into his shirt pocket for a folded bill. Placing the money on the table, he chose the king. "That should do well. Usually pretty ladies bring a man good luck."

Eliza grinned and dealt the hand. "You win," she announced.

"Told you. What's your name?"

"Eliza Yates."

"I'm John Slocum. How much longer do you have to work here tonight?"

"Another couple of hours."

"I'll be over at that table," Slocum said as he pointed to one of the nearby poker games. "Come and get me when you're free to leave. There's a game or two I'd like to teach you."

She licked her lips again and smiled. This time, Eliza didn't care how brazen she looked.

2

The rest of her time dealing faro that night dragged by slower than it ever had. All the while, she watched Slocum playing poker. He didn't seem to be doing very well, but the rest of the men at the game looked to be enjoying his company. They all laughed and joked as if they were old friends. Of course, most of that could be attributed to the money Slocum was losing and the drinks he was buying. Every so often, he would look in her direction to give her a promising smile. By the time she was free to step away from her table, Eliza was aching to cash in on that promise.

The woman who came to replace her was Mary, one of the saloon girls. She wasn't a whore as such, but her job was to make the male customers feel happy enough to keep spending their money on drinks or gambling. Every so often, Mary would accompany a particularly happy customer upstairs for a while. It was her choice, and if she refused, she was more than willing to call over Michael or James, who earned their keep by bouncing unruly customers off the floor a couple of times before tossing them out the door.

"What's got you so cheery?" Mary asked as she walked around the table to take Eliza's place.

Eliza smiled and felt her cheeks warm. "I'll be entertaining someone tonight."

"Could it be that tall drink of water playing poker? The one that's been looking over at you all night?"

"His name's John Slocum."

Mary's eyebrows darted upward. "John Slocum? I've heard of him."

"Nothing bad, I hope."

Although Mary seemed intrigued as she looked over at him, she didn't answer right away.

"Is it anything bad?" Eliza whispered urgently.

"Not as such," Mary said.

"Then what have you heard?"

"He's been working over at the mill."

For the first time that night, Eliza didn't feel a flutter in her stomach when Slocum looked over at her. "I know that much already," she said. "What else?"

"One of the other men who works at the mill . . . Henry Fitch. You know him?"

"Please, Mary. Don't drag this out."

Mary nodded and pulled Eliza away from the table so they couldn't be heard by the two customers who were sidling up to place their bets. "Nothing I've heard about him is exactly bad."

"Yes. But?"

"It's just that I heard one of the men from the mill talk about how that Slocum fella shouldn't be trifled with."

"What's that mean?" Eliza asked. "Is he dangerous?"

"He's supposed to be mighty good with that gun of his." Before Eliza could panic, Mary took hold of her by both shoulders and quickly added, "That doesn't mean you should be afraid of him. He's no outlaw. If he's making eyes at you, then you should definitely take advantage."

"I'm not going to steal his money."

Mary looked offended as she said, "How dare you imply that I would . . ."

Eliza scowled at her in a meaningful way.

"All right," Mary admitted. "I may have taken advantage of

one or two men in that manner, but that's not what I meant with Mr. Slocum. You know Nellie?"

"The . . ." Eliza stopped herself before calling the woman in question a whore. Even though that was the job Nellie held at the saloon across the street, she was a nice enough girl who deserved at least some measure of respect. "The girl with the pretty hair. I know who you mean."

"Right," Mary said hastily. "The whore. She's worked in plenty of other places in these parts, and she was quite excited when she heard John Slocum was in town. Apparently, he knows how to treat a woman."

"I guessed as much," Eliza said. "He seems very polite."

"I don't think you understand." Lowering her voice to a purring, hungry growl, she said, "He knows how to treat a woman."

"Yes." And then Eliza realized what was truly being said. "Oh!"

Now that she knew her meaning was getting across, Mary nodded. "Nellie has been with more men than she can count and she still talks about John Slocum. He curled her toes several times in one night and gave it to her like she ain't never gotten it before."

"Mary!" Eliza scolded. "That's so lewd."

"But it's true." Glancing over at the poker table, Mary said, "I was going to try and seek him out myself. Since he's got his sights set on you, I say saddle him up and enjoy the ride. Just promise me one thing."

"What's that?"

"When you're through with him, point him in my direction. Nellie never saw fit to charge him for her services, and I'd be willing to make the same exception. I also hear the pistol between his legs packs a bigger bang than the one on his hip."

"That's enough," Eliza said through a giggle. "I understand."

"You play your cards right, and you sure will understand," Mary said with a wink. "And you may not be walking straight afterwards."

Before Eliza could scold her again, one of the men at the

faro table said, "If one of you ladies would like to stop gossiping and start this game, we'd like to play some cards."

"Hold your horses," Mary said as she stepped up to the table. "You boys can give me your money soon enough. Who's going to make the first bet?"

Eliza left the other woman to do her job and moved away from the table before Rolf or any of the others in charge of saloon business noticed how long she and her replacement had been dawdling. She went to the bar and told Rolf she was leaving.

"What's wrong with you?" the bartender asked.

"Nothing. Why?"

"You just look . . . rattled. Was it because of all that yelling and carrying on Dan's wife did when she came through here? Don't fret about none of that. She won't follow through on any of the threats she's been making."

"That doesn't bother me," she quickly replied. "It's not the first time she came storming in to . . . wait. What threats?"

"Nothing," Rolf said. "Forget I mentioned it. Run along. See you tomorrow."

Dan's wife spouting off more than usual really wasn't enough to get worked up over, so Eliza let it go. While crossing the room, Eliza felt her breath come a little faster. Since Slocum's back was to her, she took a moment to make sure her dress was looking its best and her hair was situated just right. Running her tongue across her lips to keep them glistening, she approached Slocum's chair and placed a hand on his shoulder. She'd only meant to get his attention, but couldn't help noticing the firm muscles beneath his shirt.

Slocum's hand came up to rest on hers. Turning to look over his shoulder, he said, "I was starting to think you forgot about me."

"Not hardly. Are you hungry?"

"Yes," he said with a look in his eyes that spoke of more than an empty stomach.

"I know a place we can go for a nice steak."

He stood and gathered up the few remaining chips he had. "As long as I've got enough left to pay for a meal, we're doing just fine." He offered her his arm and asked, "Shall we?"

Eliza smiled warmly and wrapped her arm around his. Her smile grew warmer as she felt even more of his muscles. "We shall."

Dinner was always good at Miss Tulley's Restaurant. The steaks were thick and prepared just right. Conversation between Eliza and Slocum was limited due to her nervousness and his inclination to talk about nothing more than work at the mill and the places he'd been. Although she would have loved to hear stories about bigger, wilder towns than Bennsonn, Slocum stuck mostly to tales of saloons he'd visited and how much whiskey he'd drunk while there. Using skills she'd refined while humoring players at her faro table, Eliza nodded every so often and smiled. Like those customers, Slocum was more than happy to keep right on talking about himself.

Eliza was surprised to realize she was losing interest in Slocum. She was thinking of polite ways to excuse herself after dinner when he reached across the table to place his hand upon hers. "I've just been flapping my gums all night long, haven't I?"

"No," she said quickly. "Not at all."

"I have. Sorry about that. Why don't I take you somewhere quieter?"

"It's pretty quiet here," she said.

"But it's even better in my room at the Tall Pine Hotel."

Her eyes widened, but she tried to keep him from seeing. The Tall Pine was the fanciest hotel within a hundred miles. Built originally for the rich men who'd established the mill, the hotel now catered to merchants and land barons who came to sample the finery offered by a hotel that needed only five rooms and one customer a month to keep their doors open. Even the dinners they served to locals cost a pretty penny, but were more than worth it for those who wanted to taste delicacies they would only be able to find in places like San Francisco or New York City.

"I probably shouldn't go to your room," she whispered.

Slocum leaned forward and dropped his voice to a whisper as well. "With what I paid for the room, the management won't have a thing to say about who comes up to keep me company."

"I wasn't thinking about the management."

"What then?" he asked while rubbing her hand in a way that sent a chill along her back.

"It's just . . ." Suddenly, a thought sprang to Eliza's mind. "You work at the mill, right?"

"Just for now," he said. "And just until I move along to some other town."

"If you have enough money to pay for a room at the Tall Pine, why are you working at the mill?"

Slocum shrugged. "I had a good night at the card table. Not at your saloon, but the Axe Handle. Thought I'd treat myself. I'd like to treat you as well."

For too much of her life, Eliza had played by the rules. Most of the time, she hadn't even thought to question whose rules they were or why she should follow them. It wasn't long ago that she'd decided to follow her heart and take the reins of her life firmly in hand. It had worked out well so far. She had more interesting friends, a more interesting job, and was making enough money to stash away for the time when she would be able to pick up and go somewhere other than Bennsonn. After that happened, she wouldn't be hampered by propriety or expectations. And so, it stood to reason that she shouldn't be hampered by those things now.

Then again, there was always the distinct possibility that she was merely talking herself into something because of the way a handsome man was looking at her and what she felt when she touched him. Whichever reason was behind it, she knew what she wanted.

"Are those rooms at the Tall Pine really as fancy as they say?" she asked.

"There's one real good way for you to find out."

Eliza was certain there were plenty of reasons to refuse the offer Slocum was clearly making. At the moment, she couldn't think of a single one.

3

The first thing Eliza noticed when she walked into Slocum's room was that it was every bit as fancy as she'd been expecting. He lit one of the oil lamps on a nearby table, which gave the room a soft, warm glow. The chairs were intricately carved and padded. There was expensive-looking paper on the walls. Even the handle on the door was brass and polished to a shine. The second thing she noticed was Slocum's hands on her hips.

Eliza was startled at first, but had already given in to the moment by agreeing to come this far. Her head started to spin as she felt his mouth press against hers while she was pulled closer to him. His touch was rough and urgent as he walked her toward the bed. His hands wandered along her back to grasp her backside. Soon, she could feel his erection straining against his jeans and rubbing against her. Eliza hadn't been with many men, and she felt somewhat wicked as she reached down to stroke the growing bulge in his crotch.

"That's it," he said. "Keep at it, darlin'."

She opened her mouth and let her tongue slip into his. When she unbuckled his belt and realized it was the holster strapped around his waist, Eliza felt an excited chill run through her. The gun was heavy and she lowered it to the floor, thinking

15

about all the things it was capable of. Before she knew it, she had his pants down over his hips and was freeing his cock from his undergarments.

Suddenly, Slocum pushed her onto the bed and unbuttoned his shirt. Eliza watched him anxiously while pulling up her skirts. She gasped with excitement when he reached down to strip away the last layers of fabric to reveal the thatch of hair between her thighs. She was wet and ready for him. Her heart pounded with anticipation as she spread her legs and unbuttoned the top of her dress.

His penis was rigid when he guided it between her legs. Eliza gripped the bed with both hands and let out a moan as Slocum pumped into her. He drove into her harder with every thrust. When he lowered himself on top of her, Eliza wrapped her legs around him and said, "I want it faster."

"Yeah," he grunted. "I'll give it to you how you like it."

He pumped faster and Eliza savored every second. Lying on that unfamiliar bed with its expensive blanket and over-stuffed pillows, she was living the dream she'd had for so long about breaking free and doing whatever she pleased as long as it felt good. She smiled and let herself go even further, moaning with him and pumping her hips in time to his rhythm.

"Now," she moaned. "Slower."

Slocum wasn't listening. He pounded into her again and again. She was more than wet enough to accommodate him, but Eliza needed the change of pace to bring her climax closer to fruition.

"Slower," she urged.

Slocum pumped one last time, arched his back, and exploded inside her. After a few seconds of trembling, he rolled off her and wiped the sweat from his brow. "Bet you . . . never had it . . . like that."

Still feeling a tingle beneath her skin, Eliza rolled onto her side and ran a hand across his chest. "That was so exciting," she said.

"You're damn right it was."

"I want you to touch me some more."

"Huh?" he grunted.

She took Slocum's hand to guide it toward her breasts. Her nipples were erect and eager to feel his touch on her sensitive skin.

He couldn't pull his hand away fast enough. "Give me a minute to catch my breath, will ya?"

"I was just . . ." Seeing that she'd lost his attention, Eliza reached out to see if she could coax his penis back to its former hardness.

"What did I just tell you?" Slocum snapped as he jumped to his feet to pull his clothes back on.

As she watched him hiking his pants up while trying not to fall over, Eliza wondered if this was the same man she'd been so attracted to back at the Second Saloon. Now that she thought about it, she wondered why Mary and that other girl she'd mentioned had gone on so much about John Slocum in the first place.

"Are you angry?" she asked.

"No," he grunted. "Just tuckered out. You know how that is."

"Yes," she said, even though she had more than enough energy to rumple the bed linens a whole lot more. Then, she thought of something that gave her some hope to salvage the rest of the night. "Maybe you just need to rest. Come lie down with me."

"Nah. I'm gonna play some more poker. Maybe my same seat is still free."

Eliza stripped out of her dress and knelt on the bed facing him. Her hands wandered along the front of her body, lifting her full, rounded breasts while savoring the feel of her nipples sliding against her palms. "Come back here with me. You can catch your breath, and when you're ready, I can show you why it's so much better in here than out at any poker table."

"Can I win a fistful of money here with you?" Slocum asked.

Her hands froze in place and her smile dimmed.

"Didn't think so," he said. Walking over to the bed, he said, "Tell you what. You can wait right here if you like. When I'm through with my game, I'll come back and give you another ride. How's that sound?"

"Good. I suppose."

Someone knocked on the door.

Slocum put his hand on the side of her breast before moving it down to her hip. Giving her rump a playful swat, he said, "That's the spirit. This place has a kitchen that's the best in town." He reached into his pocket, removed some folded money, and tossed it onto the mattress beside her. "Take this and get whatever you like."

"I don't want your money! What kind of a woman do you take me for?"

Slocum shrugged as the person outside knocked again. "Then buy yourself something pretty. I should be back a little after midnight or so. If you wanna do it up right, be waiting in that bed wearing nothing but a smile. Sound good?"

Eliza stared at him, unable to put the proper words together for what she was feeling. When Slocum reached for the door handle, he grinned at her. "Don't fret now," he said while cupping the bulge between his legs. "There'll be plenty more where this came from."

"Don't talk to me like that!" she said.

Spitting out a laugh, Slocum started heading out. "You don't like it, honey? Here's the d—"

The door had barely opened a crack before it was shoved open the rest of the way with the force of a hurricane. Slocum was clipped by the edge of the door, which spun him partially around and knocked him to one side. Eliza screamed and reached for the blanket to pull it up and cover herself with the thick, downy layers.

"Hello, Lester," said a tall man who stormed in from the hall to grab Slocum by the front of his shirt.

Despite his current predicament, Slocum glanced over to Eliza and grinned uncomfortably while saying, "Lester? I don't know who that—"

Once again, he was cut off. This time, it was by a fist that slammed directly into Slocum's nose to unleash a torrent of blood flowing freely from both nostrils. A sickening crunch drifted through the air, followed by a wailing cry as Slocum twisted within the intruder's grasp like a fish dangling from a hook.

The intruder gripped Slocum's shirt with both hands and lifted him to his tiptoes. Following Slocum's line of sight, the other man spotted Eliza and said, "Get your clothes on and leave."

Eliza kept the blanket pressed against her chest as she scooted backward to climb down the side of the bed farthest from the door.

Shifting his focus back to Slocum, the other man shook him roughly and snarled, "What the hell were you thinking? Using *my* money to pay for the most expensive hotel room in town along with a whore to join you in it?"

"I'm not a whore!" Eliza said.

"Shut up!" Slocum barked.

The intruder slammed Slocum's back against a wall and then slapped his hand flat against the twisted, bloody wreck that was Slocum's nose. "Don't talk to a lady like that."

"Thank you," Eliza said.

"Even if she is a whore."

"Hey!"

Whoever the other man was, he wasn't at all concerned with Eliza's protests. For the moment, Slocum seemed to have forgotten about her as well. "Explain yourself," the intruder demanded. "And be quick about it."

Smiling through the bloody mask that was spreading to cover most of his face, Slocum said, "You know damn well what it's about. Payback!"

"Payback for what?"

"For what you took from me. You stole what was rightfully mine, so I take from you."

The intruder let Slocum go and stepped back. When his hands dropped to his sides, Eliza noticed the gun strapped around his waist. The weapon remained holstered for the time being, but the stranger's hand hung less than an inch above it like a specter of doom.

"If you had a problem with me," the stranger said, "why didn't you come and face me like a man?"

Slocum used the back of one sleeve to wipe some of the blood from his face. Wincing as he bumped his crooked nose, he replied, "You stole from me like some snake in the grass, which is how I treated you. Ain't no reason to treat a snake like a man. Just look at you now! Busting in here to hit me when I wasn't looking!"

"After what you pulled, you should have been looking over your shoulder every second. But you're too stupid for that, which is why you got caught with your pants down." Looking over at the bed, the stranger added, "Or, I should say, *almost* got caught with your pants down. Hope you enjoyed yourself with my money because the party ends right now."

Slocum licked his lips and spat blood. "That's where you're wrong, John. The party's just getting started!" With that, he raised his fists and lashed out with a vicious right cross that had more than enough steam behind it to take a man's head off. Instead, the stranger leaned back to let the fist pass in front of him before leaning right back in again to snap a jab into the middle of Slocum's bloody face.

The next several punches from Slocum were thrown in an angry flurry. Each one was delivered with more power than the one before it, but each one was farther off its mark than its predecessor. In fact, the stranger was cracking a smile as he bobbed his head to avoid one swing after the next. When Slocum tried to knock that smile from his face, the stranger ducked beneath the punch and drove his knuckles deep into Slocum's gut.

Wheezing to try and draw his next breath, Slocum shoved the stranger back to create some distance between them. "You . . . still owe me!"

"You're damn right I do," the stranger replied before surging forward to drive his shoulder into Slocum's chest. Slocum was taken off his balance while backpedaling into a small table bearing an oil lamp on its polished surface. The lamp fell to the floor, shattered, and created a small pool of fire as the wick ignited the spilled oil.

Even though it pained him to stand up straight and laugh, Slocum did just that. "Guess who's gonna pay for this, John? The fella registered to this room!"

The stranger wasn't shaken in the slightest by the flames that grew to cast flickering shadows on the walls. He placed one foot down behind Slocum's heels and gave him one jarring shove. As he fell back, Slocum tripped over the other man's foot. Having been shoved toward the little fire, Slocum's back slammed against the burning wooden planks.

"Ow! Damn it all to hell!" he hollered as he leapt almost straight up off the floor and onto his feet.

"Stop your crying," the stranger said as he grabbed Slocum once more by the front of his shirt. He picked him up a few inches from the floor and then slammed him down again. The stranger repeated that process a few more times, using Slocum's back and flailing arms to stomp out the fire before it could spread. When the flames were extinguished, the stranger lifted Slocum a bit higher before letting him go.

Slocum hit the floor hard and knocked the back of his head. "You're a crazy son of a bitch!"

"And you stole from me," the stranger said. "How big of an idiot does that make you?"

All this time, Eliza had been gathering her clothes and pulling them on. Now that she was dressed, she looked for a way to get out. There was a window behind her, but crawling out of that and dropping to street level was anything but appealing. If she was to get to the door, she needed to slip past both men as they fought. No matter how distracted the stranger might have been, she doubted he would be true to his word and just let her pass.

As if sensing the thoughts racing through her mind, the stranger turned toward her and said, "I told you to leave."

"Or what?" Slocum asked. "You gonna smack her? You gonna beat on a woman?"

"I could hear some of what you were saying before I came in," the other man said. "Not exactly the sort of talk I would call chivalrous."

"Shiv-a-what?"

"You just made my point."

Still too frightened to get any closer to the two men, Eliza found herself silently agreeing with the stranger. As she thought

back to how Slocum had been acting before the violent inter-
ruption, she couldn't help taking some amount of pleasure from
the rough way the stranger tossed Slocum to his feet and gave
him a quick jab to the stomach.

"Where's the rest of my money?" the stranger asked.

"Ain't no more," Slocum replied.

"I don't believe that. Where is it?"

"You wanna hear me say it again?"

"No," the stranger said as he shoved him against the wall.
"I want to hear you tell me where the rest of my money is. You
couldn't have spent every dime of it."

There was another knock, only this one was on the door-
frame and was considerably more timid than the one that had
announced the stranger's presence. A sweaty man with a long
face peeked into the room and said, "I must insist that you take
any trouble outside."

"We're almost through here," the stranger said. "Isn't that
right, Lester?"

Looking at the sweaty man, Slocum said, "I don't know this
man and I don't know any Lester. He's out of his head!"

"Should I get the sheriff?" the sweaty man asked.

Slocum's eyes went wide, and even though he was still being
manhandled by the stranger, he looked at the sweaty man and
said, "No! No law. Just get this maniac outta my room!"

The man in the hall looked just as confused as Eliza felt.
The only one who wasn't puzzled by Slocum's response to that
was the stranger, who had him pinned against the wall.

"What's the matter, Lester?" the stranger asked. "Afraid a
lawman will take my side instead of yours? Or maybe you're
worried that if anyone looks at your claims more than once,
they'll see right through the horse manure you've been expecting everyone to believe." Turning toward the man in the hall,
the stranger asked, "Do you work here?"

"I am the manager of this establishment," the sweaty man
proudly declared.

"Why don't you fetch the law so we can get this straightened
out?"

"Might I ask who you are?"

"Certainly—"

The stranger was cut short by a desperate, chopping blow from Slocum. His teeth were bared and his face was red, giving him the appearance of a wild man as he hit and kicked the stranger in a flurry of flailing limbs. The stranger held his ground by tucking his head down and bringing both arms up to protect himself. Even staying purely on the defensive, he was forced to absorb several impacts that slipped past his guard.

When Slocum ran out of steam, the stranger lowered his hands to reveal a menacing grin. "My turn," he said.

With that, he delivered an uppercut that had enough muscle behind it to lift Slocum off his feet. That was followed by a left, which landed in roughly the same spot. Under normal circumstances, that might have been the end of the fight. Indeed, Slocum was doubled over and breathing too heavily to be much of a threat any longer, but the stranger wasn't satisfied. He planted his feet and began punching Slocum's ribs as if he were chopping down a tree with his fists. Before long, Eliza and the man in the hall were both wincing with every impact.

"G . . . go . . ." Slocum wheezed. "Go . . . get the law!"

"By all means," the stranger said as he placed a hand flat against Slocum's chest to prop him up against the wall. "Go get the sheriff so we can get to the bottom of this."

The man in the hall was dumbstruck. Although frightened by the spectacle unfolding in front of him, he was also unable to peel his eyes away from the brutal display. When he was finally able to step back from the door, the manager was drawn to the room once again by a frantic, haggard voice.

"Get me outta here," said Slocum. "Please."

The manager peeked into the room and looked directly at Eliza. "Do you need any help, ma'am?"

"I . . . think I'm all right."

"I told her to leave a few times," the stranger said. "If she's hurt, it wasn't because of me."

"Are you hurt?" the manager asked.

Eliza had been drifting back and forth between excitement,

fear, and confusion so many times in the last several minutes that she felt as if she'd run a mile in her bare feet. Now that she'd had a chance to catch her breath, however, she felt her heartbeat slow to something less than a powerful flutter against her rib cage.

"I'm not hurt," she said.

The stranger pointed a finger at Slocum as he said, "That's a real good thing. Especially for you."

Slocum plastered a shaky grin onto his face. "I wouldn't hurt no woman! Fact is, we were having a real nice time before you came busting in. Ain't that right, darlin'?"

All three of the men looked over to Eliza, waiting for her reply.

Reluctantly, she said, "I . . . suppose so."

"There now!" Slocum declared. Turning toward the manager in the hall, he added, "I was just mindin' my own business in a room I paid for, mind you, when this here fellow comes charging in to toss me around."

"Is that true?" the manager asked.

The stranger kept his gaze locked firmly upon Slocum. "This one and I have some matters to discuss. As for the damage, perhaps he'd see his way clear to settling up without getting the law involved."

Slocum slapped at the stranger's hand without moving it away from his chest. Only when the stranger decided to let him go was Slocum able to take even one step away from the wall. Dusting himself off as if his rumpled clothing were the only thing wrong with his appearance, he said, "I don't think it's necessary to get the law over here after all."

"Are you sure about that?" the manager asked.

"Yeah."

Peering in from the hall, the manager said, "There does seem to be some damage done to the room. I'll have to insist on compensation for that as well."

The stranger smiled. "That shouldn't be a problem. Mr. Slocum here has plenty of money left over from his lucrative night at the card tables. Isn't that right?"

"Yeah."

Looking very relieved, the manager said, "Well, if that's settled, I'll let you gentlemen resolve your issues. We here at the Tall Pine pride ourselves on putting our customers first."

"A good policy," the stranger said.

"But . . . as I mentioned . . . I will need to receive compensation for damages and it will have to be in a prompt manner."

"Shouldn't be a problem. One of us will come to the desk real soon to settle up." Looking to both the manager and Slocum, the stranger asked, "That sound good to everyone?"

"Yeah," Slocum sighed.

The manager clapped his hands together and stepped away from the door. "Excellent! I'll get started on figuring up a bill for the damages, but I'll need to have a closer look at the room to determine—"

"Sure, sure," Slocum grunted as he reached out to slam the door in the manager's face. "Whatever you say."

The manager spoke a few muffled words which couldn't be heard from within the room before walking down the hall.

Keeping his hand on the door handle, Slocum allowed his head to droop. "Perhaps . . . this got a little out of hand."

"A *little*?" the stranger replied.

"You gotta admit, though . . . you started it."

"I don't have to admit a damn thing." When the stranger drew the gun from his holster, it was in a motion that was quicker than Eliza thought possible. One second, the man was standing there with his shoulders squared, and the next, he had pistol in hand and was ready to fire.

Until this moment, Eliza had only seen Slocum as a fighter. From the first time she'd laid eyes on him, he'd had an air of strength about him that she'd found appealing. Even when he'd been on the losing end of the fight with the stranger, Slocum didn't cave in. That had suddenly changed.

"It doesn't have to end this way," Slocum said in a voice that bordered on a whimper.

"I'm not the one who decided that," the stranger replied. "You did that when you stole from me."

"I know and I'm sorry. I'm so sorry. You've got to believe me."

"Doesn't take much of a man to apologize when it's the only option left to him."

"What can I do to set this straight?" Slocum asked.

"You can start by returning whatever money you got left."

Slocum dug into his pockets with trembling hands. Removing a few crumpled bills and some poker chips, he handed them over.

"Now get to the front desk and settle up whatever bill you're asked to pay."

"But I don't have the money . . ."

"I don't care what you have to do or if you have to scrub floors to make it up," the stranger told him sternly. "You'll do whatever it takes. If I find out there's an outstanding balance expected and no arrangements were set up by you or anyone else, I'll have another conversation with you that won't end as friendly as this one. You understand me?"

Looking at the gun being pointed at him caused Slocum's face to pale. Even though he still wore his own pistol strapped around his waist, he wasn't eager to reach for it. "I do," he said without moving a muscle. "Can I go now?"

The stranger glanced over to Eliza. "What about you, ma'am? Are you sure he didn't hurt you?"

"I'm sure."

"Does he owe you any money?"

"No! I'm not that kind of woman!"

"All right then," the stranger said to Slocum. "You're free to go. But remember, I can find you anytime I want."

Slocum skulked out of the room without looking back and without saying another word.

The stranger tipped his hat to Eliza. "Sorry about frightening you, ma'am."

After all that had happened, Eliza only had one question. "Who *are* you?"

"I'm the real John Slocum."

4

The real John Slocum took his time walking down the hall
to the top of the stairs that led down to the Tall Pine's impressive lobby. Although no room in the hotel was particularly large,
each was decorated with everything from brightly colored
sconces on the walls to intricately carved patterns in the ban-
isters. Thick carpets on the stairs muted his steps as he made
his way to the first floor. He was halfway down when another
set of smaller footsteps hurried to catch up to him.

"Wait right there," Eliza said as she hurried to get to Slocum
while also securing the last of her dress's buttons.

Stopping so he could see a portion of both floors, Slocum
placed a hand on the banister and waited.

Eliza seemed surprised that he'd listened to her and nearly
charged straight into him as she raced down the stairs. Having
overshot him by a step, she hopped back up so she was on equal
footing with him.

"Something I can do for you?" Slocum asked.

"You need to explain yourself!"

"Do I?" he said with a scowl on his face that still managed
to look somewhat good-natured.

"Since I was the one who was nearly killed, I'd say you most certainly do!"

Suddenly, the manager took notice of them. "We do have other guests about," he said in a hurry. "Perhaps you'd like to take your conversation to somewhere more private?"

"I could sure use a drink," Slocum said.

The manager swept his hands toward a doorway framed by thick, velvet curtains. "By all means, partake of our fine selection of wines and liquors. Your first one is on the house."

"No!" Eliza said while stamping her foot.

Slocum took hold of her arm in a gentle, yet firm grip while leading her the rest of the way down the stairs. "I think our complimentary drink is hinging on us getting out of the lobby as quickly as possible."

"The gentleman understands perfectly," the manager said. "Now, if you'll excuse me, there's still the matter of this bill to settle." He then returned to his conversation with the man who'd been bounced off walls and pummeled to the point of being tenderized.

Beyond the velvet curtain was a dimly lit room containing a short bar manned by a well-dressed fellow in a crisp white shirt. There were several small round tables scattered beneath a thin veil of smoke from expensive cigars and imported cigarettes. Not only was the hotel manager happy to signal for the bartender to give them free drinks, but he was just as eager to tug the ropes holding the curtains in place so they fell shut to close the room off from the lobby.

"What a great place," Slocum said as he escorted Eliza to a table. "Even when they're making you feel unwelcome, they're hospitable."

Eliza wanted to stay angry at him and the situation in general, but had to fight to keep her scowl in place, given her plush surroundings. "You say you're John Slocum?" she asked.

"I said it and meant it."

"Then who's the man out there? The one who was claiming to be John Slocum all this time?"

"His name's Lester Quint."

"And why would he lie about who he is?" she asked.

"Because he had an axe to grind with me and was too yellow to step up and face me like a man."

The well-dressed barkeep came over to them to ask what they wanted to drink. He also made it very clear that only their first round was on the house.

"In that case," Slocum said, "I'll have a shot of your finest whiskey."

"For you, ma'am?" the barkeep asked.

Eliza shook her head. "I don't want anything."

"You sure you want to turn down a free drink from a place this fancy?" Slocum asked.

She sighed. "I'll have some wine."

"Not just any wine," Slocum added.

"Our finest wine?" the barkeep asked.

"You got it."

Judging by the way the barkeep smirked before walking away, he wasn't at all bent out of shape about giving away some of the hotel manager's most expensive merchandise.

"I'd appreciate an explanation," Eliza said. "After all, I was almost shot back there. Not to mention the fact that I've been lied to and—"

Slocum held up a finger and angled his head toward the velvet curtain. There was a commotion brewing in the lobby, most of which came from the pounding of a fist against a desk and Lester's raised voice. "You weren't almost shot," he said. "Now listen—"

"But I don't *have* that kind of money!" Lester said from the next room.

"Then you'll have to come up with some other sort of arrangement, just as your friend suggested," the manager replied.

"He ain't my friend. At least let me have the money back that I paid for that damn room."

"Sorry, sir. Our policy is no refunds."

"I'll wring your scrawny . . . hey! Get your hands off 'a me!"

Slocum's smile widened. "I noticed a few large fellows

lurking in a back room," he said as if Eliza were in on a shared joke. "It was only a matter of time before they got called in. Should we take a peek at him getting tossed out on his ear?"

"I'm not interested in any of that," she said.

"You're right. Better to just listen to the music while sipping our complimentary drinks."

As if on cue, the barkeep walked over to place the drinks on the table. He winced at the sound of Lester being shoved, kicking and screaming, out of the hotel. Once the front door slammed loudly, Lester's voice was muffled well enough to be ignored.

"Now that," Slocum said while drinking his whiskey, "was fun. Almost worth the price I paid."

Eliza took a sip of her wine to steady her jangling nerves. It tasted so good that she had to take another. Although the wine had a definite calming effect on her, she still wore a cross expression on her face when she said, "I'm waiting for an explanation and I think I deserve one."

"That man who got booted out of here is Lester Quint, and I'm John Slocum."

"You already told me that. You also said he had an axe to grind with you. Is that what led to you busting into our room like a bull?"

After a moment's consideration, Slocum said, "Yeah. I suppose it was. You see, I've been working at the mill for a little over a month now. It's good money, honest work, and the people there are friendly. Well . . . I should say *most* of the people there are friendly. Lester and some idiots who look up to him do the least amount of work possible and then complain when they don't get any additional pay or added responsibility. They especially didn't like it when I was bumped up to an overseer for one of the saw crews."

"After only being there a month?" Eliza asked while taking another sip of her wine. "Impressive."

Slocum shrugged. "I showed up on time every day and did the best I could. To be honest, I think I was just given that position to teach Lester a lesson. He was talking to the foreman, complaining pretty loudly about some bunch of money he expected to get. Perhaps he was trying to borrow it. I don't rightly know for sure. All I know is that the foreman didn't want to give Lester whatever he was demanding. Considering the tantrum he was throwing, I doubt Lester would have been given a crumb from the floor by anyone with an ounce of dignity. He's an arrogant bastard. Pardon my language."

"It's all right," she sighed. "I haven't known him for very long and I don't have any problem imagining him throwing quite the fit."

"He threw an even bigger one when the foreman patted me on the back and rewarded me for a job well done. Could have been to set an example, but it was most likely just to get under Lester's skin. Anyway, as soon as I walked away from him, Lester comes right up to me and asks to borrow some money. The icing on the cake was when he said that I should hand over as much as he wanted since I would get plenty of money for puckering up and kissing the foreman's rump."

Eliza chuckled and shook her head. "Apparently nobody told him that one can catch more flies with honey than with vinegar."

"I had plenty of things to tell him but that wasn't one of them. Needless to say, Lester wasn't happy about being turned away twice in a row. When payday came along, everyone got their wages but me. And I had plenty more than my regular pay due. I'd been taking every odd job I could so I could stash away as much as possible. The foreman even owed me a healthy sum from a poker game the week before and was going to pay me once this payroll came in."

"Oh my. Did Lester know about all of that?"

"I doubt he's that sharp," Slocum said. "He probably just got his hands on the money set aside for me and got lucky on the rest."

"So . . . why would he claim to be you?"

"Because it's a lot better to be me than some ugly snake in the grass like him."

Eliza giggled, partially due to the wine. She took another sip and swirled the remainder around in her glass.

"Actually," Slocum said, "he got wind of a line of credit I had at the Axe Handle. The bartenders there aren't too bright, and they took him at his word when he said he was my brother."

"They just let someone come in and take your line of credit?"

"Oh, it wasn't that easy! When I went over to check on it myself, they assured me I had signed off on it. Lester signed my name and the stupid bastard didn't even spell it right. Like I said, those bartenders aren't too bright."

"How did you find out about all of this?" Eliza asked.

"It started with the person who handed out the pay at the mill. He's a good enough fellow, but was shoved around until he handed over what Lester wanted. He told the owner of the mill all about it, but it was too late. Lester was already out spending my money."

"Maybe that's why he used your name," Eliza offered. "So he wouldn't be so easy to track down."

Slocum paused and furrowed his brow. "Could be, but I still think that's giving him too much credit. Anyway, the rest was just following the trail of an idiot tossing around money like it was water. He'd been busy for the whole night without stopping to sleep."

"I imagine it was more than one night."

"Maybe," Slocum replied with a shrug. "I didn't come in to collect my money until a day after the payroll arrived. I had some business to tend to."

When Eliza thought back to the things Nellie had said in regard to Slocum's prowess with a woman, she had a fairly good idea of what some of that business entailed. Smirking while sipping at her wine, Eliza decided to keep those thoughts to herself.

"By the time I knew exactly what was happening," Slocum continued, "Lester had already spent almost all my money and spread the word around town that he was me. I came here for peace and quiet so I hadn't been giving everyone my name.

Considering some of the people who I ran into the last time I was in these parts, I'm surprised nobody put a bullet into his fool head."

"What a strange story," Eliza said.

"I've lived through stranger. Anyway, my apologies that you got caught up in all of this." Suddenly, Slocum leaned forward and looked at her with deadly serious eyes. "Did he force himself on you?"

Flushing in the cheeks, she shook her head. "No."

"Did he otherwise hurt you?"

"No, but he was . . . well . . . not quite the man I was expecting."

"Why's that?" Slocum chuckled. "Were you expecting me?"

Clearly, that question was meant as a joke, and Eliza laughed right along with him while doing her best to cover the embarrassment she felt.

"I just hope he doesn't come around looking for me," she said.

"I'll see to it that he doesn't," Slocum assured her. "Where did you meet him?"

"I deal faro at the Second Saloon."

He nodded. "I know where that is. Been in there once or twice. Since they appear to have much prettier dealers than the Axe Handle, I'll have to stop by more often."

"See that you do," Eliza said. Even as those words came out of her mouth, she was surprised by them. The boldness she'd felt before, combined with the wine, had allowed her to speak her mind without second-guessing herself. "I've heard some very good things about him. Well, I suppose I heard them about you." She placed a hand to her forehead. "This is getting confusing."

"And this," Slocum said while holding up his glass, "doesn't help very much in that regard."

She laughed some more. "No, it certainly doesn't."

"That's much better."

"What is?"

"You," he said. "A pretty lady like you shouldn't be as angry as you were before."

"Well this," she said while holding up her glass, "helps quite a lot in that regard."

"Yes it does." Slocum tossed back the rest of his whiskey and stood up. "Since I've apologized and made certain you're in a good way, I'll consider my work here to be done."

"Do you have to leave?"

"Sorry to see me go? Not too long ago you were chasing me down as if you meant to do me in."

"That was then," she said. "Now I'm enjoying your company."

"Then perhaps we should continue this some other time."

"I'd like that."

Slocum tipped his hat to her and then ducked through the velvet curtain separating the restaurant from the lobby. She heard a few uncomfortable pleasantries from the manager, followed by the sound of the front door opening and closing.

Eliza sat at her table to finish her glass of expensive wine. As she polished off the last few sips, she thought about the two John Slocums she'd met that day. Of one thing, she was absolutely certain. The second was much better than the first.

5

The first thing Slocum did when he left Eliza at her table was check with the manager at the front desk about arrangements that had been made to pay for damages done to the room. The manager wasn't happy about it, but he'd reached an agreement with Lester involving several small payments as well as Lester coming in to repair the damages himself to work off some of the debt. When the manager asked if Slocum had enough money to settle the account outright, Slocum leveled with him.

"Lester took all the pay I was supposed to get for my work at the mill," he told the man behind the front desk. "To be honest, he gouged me even more than he gouged you."

If the manager had been unhappy before, he was doubly so after hearing that.

Of the concerns he had at the moment, making that manager happy wasn't one of them, so Slocum stepped outside and put the town's fanciest hotel behind him. As he walked down the street, he felt every bit of work he'd put in over the last few days sink in at once. Not only had he been working extra duties at the mill, but he'd been tracking down Lester Quint. Even though confronting the thief was deeply satisfying, it was yet another thing to wear him down to a nub.

When he'd first arrived in Bennsonn, Slocum had been sleeping in one of the spare rooms in the back of the mill reserved for workers who needed a place to lay their heads in between paydays. After he'd scraped some money together, he treated himself to breakfast at a place called the Morrison House, which he'd passed whenever going to the stable to check on his horse. The scent of baking biscuits and frying bacon had been almost more than he could bear. Finally indulging in a meal there was one of the best experiences he'd had in recent memory. Since the Morrison House was also a boardinghouse with reasonable rates, Slocum had been staying there ever since.

At this time of night, all but one of the windows was dark. Slocum stepped onto the front porch, being careful not to put too much weight on the creaky boards, and tested the door handle. It was locked. He winced, thinking about the hell he would get after waking up the lady who ran the place so he could be let in. As he was considering how quietly he could knock out one of the windows near the door, one of the curtains parted and a cautious eye surrounded by wrinkled skin peeked out at him. Slocum waved at the sliver of a face, knowing he might still be in for some hell.

The lady who opened the door was several inches shorter than Slocum and skinnier than a scarecrow. Her black hair was drawn back into a bun, and beady little eyes scrutinized him as her mouth drew into a tight, unhappy line. "It is late," she said in a dry voice colored by a Hungarian accent.

"Sorry about that, ma'am. Couldn't be helped."

Helga Morrison was the owner of the boardinghouse and ran the place by a strict set of rules. Staying out past ten was on the long list of forbidden activities. If not for her skill in the kitchen and the softness of her mattresses, Slocum would have rented a room from a less oppressive innkeeper. "You were at a saloon?" she asked.

"Actually, I was having a drink at the Tall Pine."

Her eyebrows lifted somewhat as she opened the door a bit farther. "Really?" she asked while stepping aside so he could come in. "It is as nice as everyone says?"

"Nicer. Perhaps I could take you there sometime to make up for my rudeness."

Helga laughed and shut the door once Slocum was inside. "Oh, you do not have to do that. You were not so rude. Just late. I start to wonder about my guests when they do not show. Especially when their bill is not paid."

"I do apologize for that, ma'am," he said. "You see, my pay from the mill was stolen."

"But you have enough to eat a fancy meal at the Tall Pine?"

"That was on the house, and it was just a drink. I found the thief who took my money and tossed him out. The drink was a thank-you for cleaning up the place. If you doubt me, you can ask the manager."

She waved that aside with a little sneer, which suited her much better than the earlier smile. "I just want my money for rent."

"And I'll get it for you, I swear. In the meantime, is there anything I can do to make up for what I owe? Perhaps some chores that need to be done or work you need help with?"

Staring at him as if assessing his very soul, Helga nodded. "I can maybe think of some things. Right now, I am tired. We will talk over breakfast. You like potato cakes?"

"It's been a while since I've had those," Slocum said. "I'll see you bright and early."

Once again, she waved him off and took a candle from a nearby table so she could light her way back to her room. Since that was the single source of light in the immediate vicinity, Slocum was left in almost complete darkness. He sighed and let his eyes adjust to the scant bit of illumination provided by the moon's rays seeping in through the windows. Fortunately, he'd been staying there long enough to have a good feel for the place. He avoided most of the furniture as he made his way to the staircase. Once he was at the top of the stairs, however, he knocked his shin against a narrow umbrella stand that the old woman insisted go there instead of by the front door, where it belonged. Slocum choked back a curse while rubbing his shin and went to his room.

He wasn't there for more than a few seconds before he heard a light knock on his door. "Yeah?" he grunted.

The door was pushed open by a tall woman in her early twenties. She had long, golden hair that was kept in a single thick braid currently pulled forward to rest over her shoulder. She looked at Slocum with bright blue eyes and whispered, "Not so loud. My mother will hear."

It had been difficult for Slocum to wrap his head around the fact that Greta Morrison was Helga's daughter. With a bit of imagination, he could see something of a resemblance in both of their narrow faces, but Greta's hair and bright complexion made a comparison between the two seem more like night and day. Greta did have the same slender build, but hers was accented by firm, rounded breasts.

"Your mother is already mad at me," Slocum said. "Adding one more thing to her list won't hurt my case any."

"Then you do not know my mother." Greta stepped inside and shut the door behind her. "I was hoping to see you tonight."

"And here I am."

"I meant . . . see you when the house was empty. Everyone went away to a town meeting and I waited for you."

Allowing his eyes to wander along the smooth curves of Greta's body and the milky slope of her neck, Slocum said, "Maybe we could make up for some lost time right now?"

As he stepped forward and placed his hands upon her hips, Greta moved back and gently pushed his hands away. "Now is not the time for lost time," she said. Even though that didn't make perfect sense, the way she said it still held plenty of promise for times to come.

"I thought since you came to my room and all . . ."

"I came to make sure you were all right. I heard about how you were hunting down Lester Quint."

"You did?" Slocum asked. "So you know that thieving son of a bitch?"

"He rented a room here when he first came to work at the mill. My mother did not like the look of him and told him she had to rent his room to someone else. When he came back to see there was no one else, Lester got very upset."

"What did he do?"

"Nothing," Greta said with a smirk. "Especially when my mother pointed her shotgun at him and told him to leave."

"I always knew there was something about that old gal I liked." Slocum placed his hands upon her hips again and pulled her close. "Something other than her daughter, that is."

She smiled and tried to pull away. Since she wasn't trying very hard, Greta's movements simply made her hips shift in Slocum's hands and her body writhe against his chest. "I told you," she whispered. "Now is not the time. My mother might even know I am out of my room already."

"You're not a child, Greta. You can do what you please."

"I know that, but this is my mother's house. If you think the rules she has for her boarders are something, you should see the rules she has for me."

Slocum put his face close to hers and whispered into Greta's ear while reaching around to massage her tight, rounded buttocks through her skirts. "Then why don't you buck against the rules? Wouldn't that feel good?"

"God, yes," she purred.

And as if responding to every hushed word that passed between them, a set of methodical footsteps pounded against the stairs in the hall. Greta turned around so quickly that her braid slapped Slocum across the face. "That's her," she said in a hurried whisper. "I'll see you later."

Before Slocum could do or say anything, Greta was out of his room and shutting the door behind her. She padded down the hall as footsteps from the opposite end reached the top of the stairs. Feeling like a boy who'd been caught with his knickers down, Slocum remained perfectly still. Greta hadn't shut the door all the way, so he held it in place.

The footsteps stopped directly in front of his room, and Slocum felt a chill run down his spine. Suddenly, the notion of misbehaving with Greta wasn't so appealing. Not only did

Helga have access to a shotgun, but he knew the old woman well enough to be certain she'd use it.

"Mother, what are you doing there?" Greta asked.

Slocum could hear a grating breath, followed by footsteps that traveled a bit farther down the hall. "I should ask that to you," the old woman whispered in a way that made her voice carry almost as much as if she'd talked normally.

"I am going to my room."

"From where?"

"Honestly, Mother," Greta said. She groused a bit more, but Slocum couldn't make out much of what was being said. He was ready to write off the rest of the conversation as a scuffle between mother and daughter before he heard the latter portion of Helga's response to her.

". . . know what sort of man he is."

Slocum scowled, wondering what sort of mud was being slung at him while his back was turned. In order to find out, he eased the door open just enough for him to lean out and hear a bit more without being seen in the darkened hallway.

The only other guest in the boardinghouse was a gambler named Robert McCoy. Slocum had played cards with him once or twice and used to think that the older man from Mississippi was putting on an act when he claimed to be partially deaf. Getting others to believe something like that could be an advantage at a poker table, but McCoy didn't win nearly enough to warrant much suspicion. Helga must have believed it well enough because she didn't seem to be worried about waking him as she stood in front of the door to his room with her hands upon her hips to scold her daughter.

"I have heard some things about that man," Helga said while jabbing a finger back toward Slocum's room. "You would do well to stay away from him."

"You gossip too much," Greta said. "And those old hens you have tea with gossip even more."

"It was not from them that I hear these things. Well," Helga amended, "not all of these things. Some I have heard from Sheriff Krueger."

That sparked Slocum's interest. In fact, it took every bit of restraint he had to keep himself from throwing open his door and charging out to demand the entire story be told to his face. Fortunately, it seemed he was going to hear plenty more without having to be so forward about it.

"What did you hear that was so bad?" Greta demanded to know.

Helga dropped her voice, prompting Slocum to ease his door open and lean out.

". . . sheriff told me when he came around asking about him earlier this evening," Helga said. "He was out to kill another man in town. Did you know that?"

"Did he kill that man?" Greta asked.

"No, but there was some trouble."

"I'm sure there was a good reason for John to be upset."

"But the sheriff also told me that someone has been to town looking for Mr. Slocum," Helga continued. When she twisted around to take a quick look down the hall behind her, Slocum thought for certain he'd be spotted. The old woman held her candle, which cast a flickering light upon her wrinkled face while also making the shadows even harder to pierce from a distance. Even though she looked almost directly at him, she turned back around as if she hadn't spotted anything worth her concern.

"Those men at the mill fight and argue all the time," Greta said dismissively. "That is what men do. If John and someone else had words or perhaps fought, then the sheriff is doing his job by checking on him."

"It is more than that," Helga insisted. "The man who came to town looking for Mr. Slocum is a killer. A *paid* killer."

Now Greta looked toward Slocum's room. Whether or not she could distinguish any details past the light being cast by her mother's candle, Slocum couldn't be certain. She did appear to be somewhat concerned, however. When her mother whispered in a voice that Slocum wouldn't have been able to hear if he was two feet away from them, Greta allowed her to enter her room. The door shut and all Slocum could see after that was the dim flicker of candlelight seeping beneath the closed door.

Slocum eased his door shut and stood in the dark for a few seconds. Being in the quiet room without much of anything to occupy his senses allowed him to think clearly. One name sprang to mind upon hearing the two women talking in the hall. It was the name of a man who wanted to see him dead and had a fairly good reason for it. Until now, he'd thought Bennsonn was plenty quiet enough to remain hidden away from prying eyes. So far, the only trouble Slocum had experienced was with Lester Quint and he'd already handled that. But now this matter rose up from the recent past to try and sink its teeth into him. He'd ridden all the way to Bennsonn to wait for that storm to pass. From what he'd just heard, it seemed that very storm had found him instead.

"Damn it, Buck," he snarled under his breath. "You're gonna make me kill you, is that it?"

6

"You're killing me, John! You truly are."

It was the following morning when Slocum shrugged at a stout man with a scruffy beard. "I don't know what else to tell you, Mr. Womack. That's just the way it's got to be."

Sifting stubby fingers through his thinning hair, Womack scratched his head, which sent a fine mist of sawdust drifting onto his shoulder. He and Slocum stood outside his office in the mill. The saws were working at full capacity, which filled the entire building with the sound of iron teeth biting into solid wood. Along with that, men shouted back and forth while logs were dragged into place to wait their turn beneath the large spinning blades.

"But I just gave you that job!" Womack said. "Why would you quit so soon?"

"I'm not quitting altogether," Slocum explained. "Just turning down the promotion."

"Is it because of what Lester did? I can loan you some money until the next payday and I swear he won't be a problem again."

"Oh, I'm not worried about him," Slocum chuckled. "I just think it might be better if I stay where I was, working as nothing but another set of hands."

Womack crossed his arms and studied Slocum carefully as if he was expecting some sort of surprise. When he didn't get one, he said, "I suppose that's your choice. Hate to lose a good man, though."

"Like I said, I'm not going anywhere."

"I know, I know. I heard you the first time," Womack grunted. "You're a fine worker, so if you want to go back to splitting logs instead of overseeing the men, I won't stop you. Just promise me you'll think about reconsidering my offer."

"I will." Since there wasn't much else to say, Slocum left the disgruntled Womack to fret about hiring another overseer and found a group of men who looked like they needed help loading logs onto a cart to be brought inside.

Work at the mill was hard, yet simple. Both of those things did Slocum plenty of good. Keeping his muscles moving and sweat rolling down his face allowed him to get his blood flowing and work up a hell of an appetite. As his body strained, his mind was able to digest plenty of other things. For the moment, his main concern was what he'd overheard the night before. Although he didn't worry much about a random bounty hunter trying to cash in on his scalp, Slocum was all too familiar with one that had recently taken it upon himself to track him down. Just having Buck Oberman in the same town as him meant trouble would soon follow. Any hint of a scent he might catch would only strengthen Buck's resolve. It was only a matter of time before he caught up with Slocum, and when he did, things would get real messy real fast.

Slocum thought about this for the rest of his workday, tossing different possibilities back and forth in his mind as he carried logs, swept floors, loaded freshly cut planks, and even fixed a broken cart wheel. By the time the day was over, he wasn't certain giving his mind so much time to work on its own was such a good thing.

As he left the mill, Slocum was just one face in a sea of men heading back into town. Those numbers quickly dwindled when some of the men split off to go to their homes while others found their way to a saloon. Slocum couldn't help noticing the folks standing on the boardwalks of the main streets, watching the procession of workers. They were locals tending to their own business or possibly some family members waiting for their loved ones to return to them after a long day. Some of the folks were there almost every day. The ones Slocum didn't recognize seemed as if they were staring directly at him.

Reflexively, his hand dropped to his side but his holster wasn't in its usual spot. Management at the mill frowned upon men coming to work with guns strapped to their hips. It was a reasonable policy that Slocum understood perfectly. Today, he felt exposed and helpless. He still had a knife tucked into his boot, but that wouldn't do a whole lot of good if someone decided to take a shot at him. Simply having a gun belt around his waist was enough to make a potential attacker think twice before coming at him. Unarmed, Slocum was practically inviting an ambush.

"Aw hell," he grunted. "I'm getting worked up over nothing."

His walk back to the Morrison House took him through the town's saloon district. The Second Saloon was on his left, so he stepped in there and headed straight for the bar.

"What can I get for ya?" the barkeep asked.

"How's your beer?"

"Best in town!"

Since any barkeep worth his salt would have made the same claim no matter what sludge was mixed into the establishment's brew, Slocum wondered why he'd even bothered to ask that question. Even so, he slapped some money down and said, "I'll take a mug."

As the barkeep poured the drink, he asked, "You work at the mill, right?"

"I do. Have we met?"

"Nope. You're covered in sawdust," the barkeep said while placing the mug in front of Slocum. "That's a dead giveaway."

"I suppose it is." Slocum picked up the mug and took a drink. The beer wasn't the best he'd ever tasted, but it wasn't putrid and it did a good job of clearing the dust from his throat.

When the barkeep reached for Slocum's money, he was stopped by a sharp slap to the back of his hand. "Hey, now!" he said.

After giving him the playful slap, Eliza wagged a finger at him. "Rolf," she said, "if you take that money, you'll be getting a lot worse than that from me."

"Every man's gotta pay for their drinks," the barkeep said.

She stood beside to Slocum and rubbed his shoulder. "Not after they've saved my life."

Rolf's eyebrows went up and he nodded. "All right. But just beer." He then walked away to refill some of the glasses in front of customers at another end of the bar.

"Saved your life?" Slocum asked. "I thought you said Lester wasn't hurting you."

"He could have," she said. "He wasn't much of a gentleman." Lowering her voice, she leaned in closer to him and added, "The only way you would have gotten a free drink from Rolf after telling him anything less would be if you wrung it out of his dead body."

"No thanks," Slocum said.

"Exactly. I'm glad to see you." Examining the layer of sawdust covering his shirt, she said, "I see you're still working at the mill. Was it awkward being there with Lester after all that happened?"

"He didn't show up."

"Hmm. Imagine that. Must've crawled back under a rock somewhere."

Slocum turned to lean sideways against the bar. That way, he could take a good, long look at the woman who'd decided to join him. Eliza wore a black dress with hints of white lace in the skirt and sleeves. Though the collar buttoned all the way to her neck, there was still plenty to catch his eye. Even if she'd been wrapped in a burlap sack, he still would have noticed the slopes of her large breasts and inviting curves of her rounded hips. For the moment, though, the most captivating thing about her was the smile that positively beamed as she looked at him.

"You seem to be doing much better than the last time I saw you," he said. "I'm glad to see it."

"Funny what a good night's sleep in your own bed can do. My life may not have been in danger, but I do owe you my thanks."

"No you don't," Slocum said. "As I told you before, I was coming after Lester no matter what. He got what was coming to him, and if you happened to benefit a little along the way . . . so be it."

"Here, here!"

Slocum took another drink and then said, "Remind me again . . . how did you benefit exactly? Because if he did hurt you or was about to and you didn't tell me, then I'd like to have another word with Mr. Quint."

"I told you all there was to tell," she assured him. "The more I thought about how that man lied to me to get what he wanted, the angrier I got. What I got out of you busting into that room was getting to watch as he was taken down a peg or two by having the tar beaten out of him. There are plenty of men like Lester around, and it's a rare thing for a woman to see that kind of justice done."

"Well then, I'm glad I could oblige. You need anyone else like Lester to be taught a lesson, you just let me know. I'll do damn near anything for free liquor."

She laughed and ran her fingers through her hair while brushing her fingertips lightly against one ear. As he watched her, Slocum couldn't help noticing just how smooth the nape of her neck was and how enticing the two little beads of sweat were as they rolled down her neck on their way beneath the front of her dress.

"I just thought of something," he said.

"What's that?"

"You were in that room under false pretenses with Lester."

"Yes," she replied. "But we established that a while ago."

"We did, but that's when I was preoccupied with the business that brought me to the Tall Pine. There's still the business that brought you to the Tall Pine that night."

Eliza winced and turned slightly away from Slocum. Because of the paleness of her skin, even the slightest flush in her cheeks was easy to spot. With the amount she was blushing at the moment, however, Slocum would have been able to spot it if her skin was as dark as a Cherokee squaw's.

"You know all too well what I was doing there," she said in a low voice.

"That's right, I do," Slocum replied. "You were there to share a bed with John Slocum."

"Please don't embarrass me."

As much as Slocum wanted to continue, if only to see how red her face could get, he grinned and said, "All right. I'll ease up."

"Thank you."

"But you'll have to do something for me."

"Don't forget the free drink," she reminded him.

He lifted the mug, toasted her, and took another long pull of the adequate brew. After wiping the foam from his mouth with the back of his hand, he said, "Then perhaps what I mean is there's something I might be able to do for you."

"You've done more than enough. Now, if you'll excuse me . . ."

Slocum took hold of her arm in a grip that was firm without being forceful and just enough to keep her from getting too far away. When he pulled her closer, she didn't do a thing to stop him.

"I have a job to do," she said. But even as she protested, her eyes betrayed a glint of excitement and her lips remained slightly parted as if she was thinking about something she wanted to taste.

"If your job is to convince new customers to visit your faro table," Slocum said, "then you're doing it real well."

She smiled and shifted on her feet. When Slocum released her arm, she stayed put and said, "Thank you."

"What I meant in regards to your business at the Tall Pine," he said in a voice that wouldn't carry any farther than the two sets of ears it was meant for, "is that you were there because Lester convinced you he was John Slocum. There was no way for you to know he was lying, and even if you did know, you're a grown woman who can do what she pleases with whomever she pleases."

"You're right about that," she said while holding her head high.

"It just seems to me that you got the short end of the stick." With a grin, Slocum added, "Of course, you would know that better than me. I never got a look at Lester's stick."

Eliza flinched as if Slocum had kicked a hole in the bar. Even after looking around to ensure nobody in the vicinity was offended by his comment, she still acted as if they were both on display. "That is a very crude thing to say."

"It is? Well, then I should try to come up with new words to use for what I want to say next." After taking a moment to make a show of mulling something over, he said, "I think I should be given the opportunity to repair any damage done to my good name."

"I believe you did that when you thrashed Lester Quint."

"I don't care about him. I want to make certain you have the right face in mind when you think of the name 'John Slocum.'"

"Don't worry about that," she told him. "I've got the right face in mind as of right now. I should get back to my table before I get in trouble."

He nodded and raised his mug. "Thanks again for the beer."

"Anytime."

Slocum let her get a few steps away from the bar before he said, "I'd like to see you again."

Pointing to the faro tables, she said, "You know where to find me."

Eliza turned her back to him and crossed the room to her table. Although some of her regular customers took notice of her return, they weren't the first to meet her there.

"Who's that?" Mary asked as she hurried over.

"That," Eliza said, "is the real John Slocum. I wish you would have been able to spot him before."

"I told you what I heard about him came from a friend of mine over at the Axe Handle. I'd never laid eyes on the man." Mary looked over her shoulder toward the bar and then quickly turned back again. "But he's sure laying eyes on you."

"Is he still looking at me?"

"If he was staring any harder, he'd burn holes through your dress. Then again, seeing as how you cut loose before, you might enjoy that sort of thing."

Eliza swatted Mary's shoulder and said, "That's enough of that talk! You cut loose all the time and it never turns into such a production."

"I've never had a night with a man that wound up with another man dragging him out by the scruff of his neck and whipping him like a dog."

"That's not exactly how it went," Eliza said.

"From what I heard, it was close." Mary looked over to Slocum and waved. "You shouldn't turn your nose up at a man like that. Take too long to think it over and I may just swoop in and steal him from you."

7

Slocum spent the next two days lost in his work. Since he'd found a way to keep his mind as well as his hands occupied with simple tasks required by the mill, those days moved fairly quickly. While the labors he needed to do were tedious and put almost as many blisters on his hands as they did his feet, the repetition allowed him to fall into a continuous rhythm that was, in many ways, restful. He could let go of his concerns and just think about the next simple task that needed to be done. When a team of two horses pulled a cart up to the large double doors at the side of the mill's main building, Slocum figured it was time to unload another bunch of freshly cut timber.

"Quick! Quick!" shouted the cart's driver. "Someone get a doctor! These men need help!"

Snapping out of the almost hypnotized state he'd been in, Slocum rushed over to the cart. The driver had already climbed down from his seat and was hurrying around to the back. By the time Slocum got there, three other workers were crowding in to get a look inside. Two men lay in the back of the cart. One was on his back and the other lay on his stomach. Both were a mess of blood-soaked clothing and shredded flesh.

Although the driver had gotten to them first, he scarcely

knew what to do for either of the bloodied men once he was there. He'd climbed into the back of the cart with them, only to stand while looking down and placing trembling hands upon the tops of their heads. "I . . . I don't know what to do for 'em," he said. "I don't even know if they're still breathin'! Someone help me."

Since the others around were only gawking at the gruesome spectacle, Slocum pushed them aside so he could climb into the cart. The driver was rattled to the core and shaking like a leaf, but this wasn't Slocum's first time wading through so much carnage. Placing a hand on the wounded men's necks one at a time, he soon declared, "They're both alive. Help me strip off their shirts."

At first, it was difficult for Slocum to tell where the men's shirts ended and their flesh began. There was so much blood soaked into the material that it all felt like strips of pulp plastered onto them. He and the driver gingerly peeled the torn strips of cotton and denim away as the men flinched and twitched every time they were touched.

"Try to sit still," Slocum said, even though he doubted either of the wounded men could hear him. "We just need to get a look at you."

Outside the cart, more workers had gathered. The ones closest to the bloody mess strained to get a closer look, and the ones behind them fought to see past the men in their way.

Now that he'd pulled some of the clothing away, Slocum could get a better look at the damage that had been done. The driver straightened up, looking down at the men before staring at the bloody strips of fabric dangling from his hands. "Jesus Christ almighty," he gasped.

"What happened?" Slocum asked.

"I don't know. I found 'em on the side of the road."

"What did this to them?"

"No idea. They didn't say anything. They were just screamin'," the driver said.

"Damn right they were screamin'," one of the nearby workers said. "They been ripped to shreds."

Slocum wheeled around to address the worker who had spoken as well as any others within the sound of his voice. "Shut up! All of you! This isn't a sideshow. If you can't help, then step back and find someone who can. Is there a doctor around here?"

One of the men nodded. "There's a doctor nearby. I think someone already went to fetch him."

"If you're not sure, then you go fetch him." When the man remained frozen in his place, Slocum barked, "Go!"

Not only that worker but two others bolted away from the cart to race toward town.

Slocum bent down to get a closer look at the man who was lying on his stomach. That one's back had been ripped open in several places. Some cuts were too shallow to be concerned about while others went so deep that muscle and bone were exposed to the light of day. The edges of most of the wounds were flayed and tattered. Dirt was stuck to the interior of most of the wounds, making the man look more like he'd been dragged behind the cart instead of riding inside it.

"What happened to these men?" Slocum asked.

"They were attacked."

Snapping his head up to look at the driver, Slocum said, "I can see as much for myself! I got eyes. Who attacked them?"

The driver shook his head. He was already dazed, and the more he looked at the blood-soaked mess in the cart, the farther away he seemed to drift. Slocum stood up and grabbed the front of the driver's shirt as he spoke in a voice that he hoped would cut through the haze gathering within his spinning head. "You did good to get them here," he said in the calmest tone he could manage. "There's more help on the way. Until it gets here, you've got to talk to me. Understand?"

Slowly, the driver nodded.

"Start from the beginning then. Tell me what happened."

"I was headed out to collect some tools that were left at the spot where the last group of trees were cut down."

"Where?" Slocum asked.

"Fall Pass." Now that the driver was looking at something

other than the bodies he'd found, his thoughts seemed to come to him with more clarity. "Last time the men were cutting out there, it was getting dark and rain clouds were moving in. We wanted to get the timber moved before it got soaked through."

Trying not to lose his patience, Slocum nodded. "All right. The men left their tools and you needed to gather them up."

"That's right."

"So you rode out there and . . . what did you see?"

"I heard wailing," the driver said.

"You heard these men screaming?"

"No," the driver said while shaking his head erratically. "I mean . . . I heard screaming as well, but the wailing caught my attention first. It wasn't like anything I ever heard before."

"An animal," Slocum said as he shifted his attention down to the man who was lying on his back. Almost immediately, he was pulled up again by the driver.

"It wasn't no animal I ever heard before," the driver said. "And I heard all there is that lives and breathes in them woods. I was a trapper long before this mill was built. I can recognize bears by the sound of their steps and wolves by their scent. This wasn't nothing like them. The stink in the air was . . . horrible."

Stooping down to examine the other wounded man, Slocum peeled away some of the clothing to find a similar terrible story etched into that man's body. "Did you get a look at whatever it was?"

"No. I just heard it."

"What about tracks?" Slocum asked. "Bits of fur. Scat in the brush. Anything at all that could tell you what this thing was or where it went. Did you see any of that?"

The driver blinked as if he'd just been splashed by cold water. Sobered by thinking along more familiar lines, he said, "No. I didn't take the time to look for any of that. These men were screaming and hurt so badly that I just got them loaded up into this here cart so I could bring 'em back here."

"You loaded them up on your own?"

Blinking some more, the driver looked back down the road

from which he'd come. "No. I wasn't on my own. Abner was out there as well! Oh God! He's still out there!"

"Abner? Abner who?"

"That'd be Abner Woodley," Mr. Womack said as he forced his way through the considerable crowd that had gathered around the cart. "He was out there scouting for the next batch of timber to be cut down. Been doing that for years . . . among other things."

"I didn't want to leave him there," the driver insisted. "He helped me get these men loaded and refused to come along. Said he'd only be slowing the cart down."

"Was that animal or whatever it was that hurt these men still out there when you drove off?" Slocum asked in a tone that was a bit harsher than he'd intended.

The driver shook his head meekly. "I can't say for certain. I imagine so. Abner said something about going after that thing as well."

Mr. Womack, the mill owner, walked up to the gathering. "You did the right thing by getting here as quick as you could," he said to the driver. "Now I want all of you men to step away from this cart!" The men responded to the sound of their boss's voice out of pure instinct and moved back. Turning again to the driver, he asked, "Can these men be moved out of there?"

"I'll need some help, but yes."

"You've got plenty of extra hands." Womack gathered up enough men to carry the wounded out of the cart and into the bunkhouse behind the mill. Slocum joined in the effort.

"I want some clean clothes, blankets, anything at all that can be used as dressing for them wounds," Womack continued as the injured men were carried along. "Doc Reece will need all he can get and I don't want him to have to wait for anything. Speaking of which, let's gather up some water or anything else you think those men might need."

Slocum helped carry the man with the majority of his wounds on the front of his body. Before making it halfway to the bunkhouse, the wounded man started to squirm and groan in agony. Hearing his suffering was bad enough, but the blood covering every inch of him made it difficult to maintain much of a grip. It was all Slocum could do to keep his hold before finally reaching the first room in the bunkhouse. The men carrying the other wounded fellow arrived at about the same time, and Slocum directed them to set the men down as gently as possible.

Along the way, he could tell that both men's wounds covered more than half of their bodies. There were cuts and scrapes all over them, but not nearly as serious as the side that had been visible at first glance. The driver was one of the men helping Slocum and he could not stop babbling for the duration of the entire walk.

"Oh my Lord," he sighed. "I'm so sorry. I'm so sorry. Please forgive me."

"Take a breath," Slocum said. "You may have saved these men's lives."

The driver nodded, but didn't seem to take much comfort from those words.

Once both men were lying on beds and several other workers had scattered to collect the things Womack had requested, Slocum placed an arm around the driver's shoulders and led him outside, where the air was a whole lot fresher. He pointed him away from the cart and most of the crowd so the main thing in the driver's line of sight was the surrounding woodlands. There was a barrel of water nearby and Slocum went to it so he could scoop up a drink with the tin dipper and bring it over to where the driver stood trembling.

"Here," Slocum said while handing the dipper over. "Take this."

When the driver didn't make a move to accept the dipper, Slocum snapped his wrist to splash the water into the other man's face. That yanked the driver out of his own thoughts and dropped him squarely back into the present.

"There you go," Slocum said while slapping the driver's back. "Looks like you're with me now."

"Yeah," the driver said as he wiped some of the water from his face. Rather than flick the water from his hands, he pushed it up over his eyes and shoved his hat back to clean off his dusty forehead. "That's a whole lot better. Much obliged."

Slocum dipped the dented cup into the water barrel once more and offered it to him. "You want this water inside you or outside?"

Taking the dipper from him, the driver said, "Inside will do nicely." With that, he drank every drop of the water in one series of prolonged gulps. He handed the dipper back, waited for it to be refilled, and then drained it one more time.

"All right," Slocum said. "Now that you're calmed down a bit, why don't you tell me the rest of what happened out there?"

"Not a whole lot else to tell. It was terrible . . . just terrible."

"Did you see anything alongside the road? Anything at all that could have been the thing that ripped those men apart?"

The driver thought about it for a few seconds before shaking his head. "Not that I can recall. Like I said, I heard that wailing and then the screams."

"What sort of wailing? Could it have been a man?"

Although the driver's first reaction was a shake of his head, he had to admit, "I suppose . . . there's a chance it could have been a man. I've heard animals that sound like men and men that sound like animals. Damn it all to hell, I'm not one bit of help."

"Those men you brought all the way back to where they can be seen by a doctor would tell you different," Slocum assured him. "Just as soon as they get the care they need. In the meantime, try to think of anything you can, anything at all, that might be a help. I know you're plum rattled right now, but this is when the memories will be freshest."

The driver nodded. "I know. I know. Just give me a second."

Womack approached them with his hands on his hips and sweat pouring down his face. "I swear I haven't moved around so much since I was one of the boys dragging logs from one spot to another."

"How are those men doing?" Slocum asked.

"As good as can be expected under the circumstances. They're still breathing, which is saying a hell of a lot."

"How long will it take for the doctor to get here?"

"Shouldn't be long at all," Womack said. "He's been called on several occasions when men get too close to the saw or get crushed beneath a piece of timber. Had one fella trip over his own two feet and split his head open on another man's boot. Any of them times, Doc Reece was here quicker than two shakes of a lamb's tail."

"Good to know," Slocum said. "Although it doesn't say much for you being able to keep your men in good health."

"Ain't none of them was my fault." Looking to the driver, Womack asked, "How's this one holding up?"

"The bushes!" the driver blurted out.

Womack cocked his head like a dog that had just heard a distant whistle. "Pardon me?"

The driver snapped his fingers and looked at Slocum as if he wasn't even aware anyone else was standing there. "I remember something now! There was something in the bushes when I was helping to drag those men into the cart. It was something big."

"How big?" Slocum asked.

"Bigger than a man. Maybe not as big as a bear."

Womack scowled. "So you don't think it was a man?"

"No, sir, I don't."

Nodding, Womack gave the driver a reassuring pat on the back. "Why don't you go into the bunkhouse and rest for a spell? Me and the rest of the boys can handle things from here. You did real good by taking care of those two. Now take care of yourself before you fall over."

The driver's smirk was tired and shaky. "I do feel like I'm about to drop. I just don't wanna turn my back on anything else that needs done."

"Don't worry about that. There'll be more to do, and when you're needed, I won't have any compunctions about asking for help."

"Thanks, Mr. Womack. Guess I'll have that lie-down."

After the driver walked away, Womack looked over at Slocum and said, "He's delirious."

"You saw those two men," Slocum replied. "Does it seem so far-fetched that something big attacked them?"

"No, but he's imagining things where the rest is concerned.

It was probably some crazed mountain man or trapper that lost his mind after being in them woods for too long."

"You don't think it was an animal?"

Womack shook his head. "Any animal that would have torn those men up like that would have done so for a reason. It would have tried to make a meal out of those two or dragged 'em off somewhere to save for later."

"Could be the horses and cart scared it away," Slocum offered.

"Could be, but I've done some hunting and have found it takes a bit more than riding down a road to frighten anything other than a rabbit or deer. Something as vicious as whatever tore up those two would have stood its ground or stayed to protect its kill."

"A man, then. I don't know if that's better or worse."

"Whatever the hell it was, it don't get to tear apart two of my men and live to see another sunrise."

8

It was early evening, and in a rare turn of events, nobody was leaving the mill. Instead of heading home or finding a saloon, the men covered in sawdust all gathered in the back of the mill, where Womack kept his office. There were almost enough bodies crammed inside those walls to fill the spacious building. Some men were even leaning against the saws themselves as if being around them for so long had robbed them of all fear of those plentiful metal teeth. They talked to each other in a low murmur, crossing their arms and shifting on their feet until Womack himself emerged from his office.

The boss of the mill had to motion only once or twice to get the quiet he was after. Stepping onto an empty crate so he could look out at all the faces gathered in front of him, he gripped the lapels of his waistcoat and spoke in a booming tone. "First of all, I want to thank you men for staying after quitting time. I know most of you have families to get to and the rest have better places to be than here, so I'll make this brief."

"Are them fellas dead?" one of the workers shouted. After he spoke up, plenty of others had things to say.

"I heard they was mauled by a bear!"

"I heard it was a band of outlaws lookin' to shut the mill down."

"I heard that driver killed 'em on account of money he was owed."

"That's enough!" Womack shouted. "I don't give a damn about what any of you heard or any stories that are floating around. The reason I called this here meeting is to tell you what I know for certain."

It took a few seconds, but the crowd simmered down and waited intently for the boss's next words.

"All right," Womack said. "That's better. First of all, I'll have you know that Doc Reece has seen to both of those men that were hurt and is doing the best he can for them. Dave Anderson is a tough son of a gun and it looks like he should pull through. Edgar Fuller was hurt much worse. As of now, he's hanging on but things don't look so good."

Slocum stood near the front of the crowd. Although he hadn't known about how the two victims were doing, he wasn't surprised by the news. Dave Anderson was the one who had most of his slash wounds on his back and shoulders. They were ugly, but didn't get much past the bones protecting his vital areas. Edgar Fuller was the man who'd received most of his wounds on the front of his body. Although his rib cage might have protected some of his innards, his belly was soft and exposed to some of the worst damage. Slocum was no doctor, but he knew a life-threatening wound when he saw one and poor Edgar had plenty of them.

"As for any accusations being leveled at Rob Ploughman," Womack continued, "you men can just put those to rest. He did his best to save two lives by getting them loaded onto his cart and bringing them here despite the danger that he was in."

Slocum nodded along with most of the rest of the crowd. It wasn't until things had settled down around the camp that he'd even caught the cart driver's name. He stored it away in the back of his head for whenever he got the chance to buy Rob a drink.

"I know the question on everyone's mind is what exactly happened to those two men out on Fall Pass," Womack said. "I'm here to tell you that that's exactly what I intend on finding out. All I know for certain about what happened . . . all any of us knows for certain . . . is that those men were brutally attacked. I'm sure that doesn't set well with many of you and I guarantee it sets with me even worse! I intend to find out what happened to my men and our friends, and I'm not going to wait around to do so!"

That sparked a loud chorus of cheers from the crowd. Slocum shared the sentiment, but stood by quietly to wait and see where Womack was headed next.

"First of all," Womack said, "I will see to it that someone is sent out to put an end to that vicious killer, whether it be man or beast. I've already spoken to Sheriff Krueger and he assures me he'll be looking into the matter."

Although some of the men in the crowd were glad to hear that, most were either quiet or voiced some discontent. Slocum was one of the quiet, albeit discontented, ones.

Seeing that he'd already lost a good portion of his admirers, Womack added, "Rest assured, if I don't get some sort of satisfactory course of action from the law, I will take matters into my own hands!"

Once again, the majority of the crowd was back on Womack's bandwagon. Many of them even shouted to be a part of whatever their boss had in mind. Slocum, on the other hand, remained quiet. He was uncomfortable at what he was fairly certain was a spur-of-the-moment statement from a man who was just trying to regain the favor of a bunch of discontented workers.

Womack nodded and motioned for quiet, which he got almost immediately. "For the moment, I ask that you men just go about your jobs and keep the wounded men in your prayers. As soon as I have anything else to report, I'll let you know by either calling another meeting like this one or posting it on the board outside my office. Now I'm sure you all would like to get away from this mill for the day so I'll see you tomorrow, bright and early. I appreciate your time." With that, Womack tossed the crowd a wave and hurried into his office so he could shut himself in.

The crowd grumbled among themselves before slowly making their way for the doors. From what Slocum could hear, most of what was being said was in Womack's favor. There were still plenty of rumors being passed around, which wasn't a surprise.

The only way to keep folks from telling stories about one another was to knock their heads together hard enough to put them to sleep. When they woke up and started wondering about who'd put them down, they would have to be knocked again.

Slocum started looking for a relatively clear path to the door through the mass of workers when he heard a hissing sound coming from the smallest room in the mill.

"Pssst! John."

Even though he was looking directly at the source of the voice, all Slocum could see was the wall of Womack's office and a door that was cracked open barely enough for light to pass through.

"John," Womack whispered again. "Get in here. Please!"

Most of the workers were satisfied with what they heard and anxious to leave for the day. Although a few of them noticed Slocum stepping into the boss's office, nobody felt compelled to force their way in behind him. Judging by the harried expression on Womack's face, one might have thought he was single-handedly holding back a siege.

It wasn't the first time that Slocum had been inside Womack's office and yet, somehow, he was still taken aback by how small it was. Compared to the wide-open space of the mill's main floor, the office wasn't much more than a closet with a few chairs and a desk crammed into it. At the moment, there was a pair of whiskey bottles in there as well.

"Needed some liquid courage to make your big speech?" Slocum asked while pointing at the bottles.

"Oh, those," Womack said. "I did take a sip or two from one of them, but the other was for Rob. He was so rattled that he drank damn near half that bottle on his own before I took it from him."

"I suppose you shouldn't let him drive another cart for a while."

"No worries there. He could barely stand when I left him. Still shaking, though. Even after he passed out. Strange."

"Considering what he saw," Slocum said, "not so strange."

"Yeah. I suppose you're right."

"So what did you want to talk about? As you mentioned a couple of times, we do have other places to be apart from this mill."

"I was hoping you might sign on to be on the party going out to get a look at whoever it was that attacked those men. I've, uh, heard a thing or two about you. Nothing terrible, mind you! Just that you were . . . are . . . handy with a gun."

"Did you hear I was a bear hunter?" Slocum asked.

"Well . . . no."

"Then I suggest you leave that sort of work to men who are."

"I still don't think it was any sort of bear that attacked those men," Womack insisted. "If it was, there wouldn't be much left of them. At the very least, they'd be missing an arm, a leg, even an eye."

"So you don't think those men were mauled *enough*. I wouldn't let that one slip at your next town hall meeting," Slocum said with a wry grin.

Womack started to say something, but cut himself short in favor of grabbing one of the bottles and pouring a finger of whiskey into a glass that was also sitting on his desk. After downing the whiskey in one swallow, he put the glass down and looked at Slocum. "You wouldn't be the first gunman to come to Bennsonn in search of some peace and quiet. We've had some infamous sorts come through here, looking to lay low and more than one of them have worked here at this very mill."

"So I'm infamous now?"

"Why are you making this so difficult for me, John?"

Slocum walked over to the desk, found a glass, and poured some whiskey for himself. "Maybe it's because of that speech you gave."

"You didn't approve?"

"I thought it was fine . . . right until the part where you promised a crowd of angry men that you'd be willing to take the law into your own hands. I can tell you from experience, that never works out very well."

"I might have spoken out of turn there," Womack admitted. "But I meant every word. Something needs to be done."

"So go see the sheriff. Hell, if you don't like what the sheriff says, there's also a marshal in town."

"Already paid the marshal a visit."

"And?" Slocum asked.

"And he told me that hunting wild animals isn't his job. When I told him men were hurt and there could be more blood spilled, he said that was a town matter."

Slocum gritted his teeth. It was bad enough that he heard about a response like that from a lawman. What made him even angrier was that the response really wasn't much of a surprise.

"One of the things I heard about you was that you've ridden on more than your share of posses," Womack said. "I'm hoping you might be able to lend me a hand in dealing with Sheriff Krueger."

"What do you want me to do where the sheriff is concerned?"

"If the sheriff has heard the same things as I have," Womack explained, "then he might be impressed with you accompanying me to see him on this matter. He also might be more inclined to send some men out to Fall Pass if he knows he's got some good shooters along for the ride."

"Meaning me," Slocum said.

"Well . . . yes. That was another thing I wanted to talk to you about. If even a few of the things I've heard about you are true, then you would be one hell of an asset to any bunch of men that went out there. If it was a man that tore up Edgar and Dave, they'll pose a threat to anyone else coming around looking for them. If it was more than one man, there could be even worse trouble. Hell, even if it's an animal, you would only improve the odds of a hunting party coming back in one piece. No matter who puts the group together, I'd like to personally ask that you be a part of it."

Slocum thought about that for a few seconds.

Uncomfortable in the short silence, Womack added, "I can pay you, of course."

That wasn't what Slocum had been thinking about, but he didn't see any reason why Womack should be told about that.

"I could use some money to make up for what Lester took from me."

"I thought you found him and . . . well . . . dealt with him," Womack said.

"I did find him, but the asshole pissed nearly every cent away in less than a day and a half."

"That's a shame. But . . . I suppose he won't be, um, bothering anyone any longer."

"Why are you squirming so much?" Slocum asked. After studying him for another second or two, he said, "You think I killed him!"

"No . . . I . . . well . . . is that such an unreasonable assumption?"

Despite wanting to defend himself, Slocum only had to think about what had happened and how close he'd been to actually putting Lester out of his misery when he did find him. "I guess it's not unreasonable, but I didn't kill him."

"Well, I haven't seen hide nor hair of him and there's been talk."

Slocum shook his head and sighed. "People and all their goddamn talk."

"Be that as it may, what do you say to my original proposition?"

"I'll go with you to have a word with the sheriff if you think that'll help. I'm curious to see what he has to say on the matter."

"I do think it'll help," Womack said excitedly. "I honestly do."

"What about that other man?" Slocum asked. "The one he left behind so he could bring those other two back here. You didn't mention him in your speech."

"No, I didn't. Mostly because all I know about him is that he's still out there. As to what condition he's in, or even if he's alive or dead, is anyone's guess. He's the reason why I wanted to talk to you in private instead of putting you on the spot when I was addressing the men." Seeing the stern glare he got from Slocum, Womack shrugged and added, "I thought that might increase my chances of you agreeing to take the job."

"Go on."

"His name is Abner Woodley. He's a good man and a hell of a hunter. He knows these woods like the back of his hand, which is how he's been able to find the best timber that's easiest for us to haul back after it's cut down and—"

"He's a valuable worker," Slocum cut in. "Move along."

"Quite simply, he needs to be found." Following Slocum's advice, he moved along. "I wanted to try and focus on the positive. Those men saw a lot of blood today. They're mill workers and lumberjacks, not soldiers. They were shaken up, and if they get too shaken up, they might think twice about working here."

"Ahh," Slocum said. "So that's it. You didn't want to scare anyone away."

"You're damn right I didn't and I don't think I need to apologize for that! This mill provides a lot of jobs and money to this town. If something happens to cripple that, there could be serious repercussions!"

Slocum held up his hands. "No need to get all worked up. I agree on that point."

"Oh. All right, then. The other thing . . . and this is a delicate matter . . . is that Abner needs to be found, even if he's dead."

"That could be tricky. If it was an animal, there might not be much left."

Some of the color drained from Womack's face, but he soldiered on. "If there are only . . . remains"—he gulped—"those need to be found, too. And buried. Out in the woods. Where . . . nobody can find them."

"Did he have a family?" Slocum asked. "They should know if he's dead. Letting folks stew about something like that isn't proper by a long shot."

"I agree, but he didn't have a family. He spoke of a brother out in Mississippi, but they weren't on speaking terms. The only reason I broach such a gruesome subject is because it ties back to what I said about keeping this mill running. The men are already speculating about what could have torn up Edgar and Dave that way. Rob isn't helping much by telling stories that just get wilder each time someone asks him about it."

Womack poured himself a drink, but didn't toss it down right away. Instead, he swirled the whiskey in his glass and watched it churn. "When those men go out into the woods, they have to contend with all manner of things. Usually just critters or whatnot, but there's also things out there that will kill them in some very unpleasant ways."

"There aren't many pleasant ways to be killed," Slocum said. "Although there was this whore in New Orleans who robbed a man after she rode him so hard that he was too tired to fight back. Killed a few when they were asleep, too. They were buried with smiles on their faces."

Womack chuckled at that and seemed even more at ease than when he'd swigged his whiskey. "My point is there are already enough things to be scared of in this world. I hate to say this, but if Abner is dead, he's already through. Letting anyone else get a look at whatever is left after that thing is through with him will only add fuel to the fire. It will give the men something terrible to add to their stories, which were already terrible enough."

Slowly, Slocum nodded. "I understand what you're saying. You're right. It is terrible, but chasing men away from good jobs and jeopardizing the main source of income for a good town are even worse."

"So you'll take the job?"

"Will I have anyone going out there with me?"

"I have a few men in mind. That is . . . unless you'd rather work alone."

"I've done a fair amount of hunting," Slocum said. "But if you have someone who can handle themselves and knows those woods, it would make things a whole lot easier."

Womack smiled broadly. "Then the men I have in mind should work out just fine! I can introduce you to them now, if you like."

"Why don't we pay a visit to the sheriff first? It could very well be that he's forming a posse and has this whole matter well in hand already."

"Oh. Right. Let's go see the sheriff."

Womack looked about as hopeful for that option to pan out as he was for chunks of gold to start raining down from the sky. Although Slocum had made the suggestion, he felt pretty much the same way.

9

The outside of Sheriff Krueger's office looked more like a cozy little home and the inside wasn't much different. Slocum had known a few lawmen who slept in the same place where they conducted their business, but they didn't normally seem so comfortable. There were two rockers on the front porch and dark green curtains in the windows. Upon entering, Slocum and Womack found themselves in a sitting room with a desk on one side and a fireplace on the other. The bookshelves were nicely stocked and the furniture was well maintained. All that was missing was the scent of freshly baking bread wafting in from the kitchen.

Krueger was a man in his early fifties with a ring of gray hair going around the back of his head and droopy eyes that made him look like he was part hound dog. When he saw the two men enter his office, he stood right up and extended a hand in greeting.

"Well, hello there, Phil!" he said to Womack. "Long time, no see!"

"Hello, Sheriff."

"Who's this you brung along with you?"

"This is John Slocum."

Krueger's handshake was firm and kept Slocum's hand trapped for a bit longer than it had Womack's. The sheriff's eyes narrowed as he gazed intently at Slocum's face. "Now why does that name sound familiar?" the lawman wondered. "Did you bring in those rustlers that were cutting a trail across Montana?"

"I sure did," Slocum replied.

"That was a nasty bit of business. Read about it in the newspapers. Five men wound up dead, one of them a U.S. marshal if I recall."

"Yeah, it got pretty ugly."

"But you got those rustlers, so that's the important thing!"

Slocum was finally able to reclaim his hand from the lawman's grip. "Losing that U.S. marshal was a terrible thing. The rest . . . well . . . at least it's over."

"This one's modest," Krueger said to Womack. "I could sure use three just like him working for me as deputies!"

"Actually," Womack said with a cheerful disposition, "that's along the lines of why we're here."

"Is it? Have a seat and tell me about it."

Slocum was already anxious when he walked to the sheriff's office and all these pleasantries weren't helping. Still, this was Womack's show and he seemed to have a good history with the sheriff so Slocum allowed things to play out for the time being.

Womack sat down in one of the chairs near the sheriff's desk while Slocum remained standing. "Perhaps you've heard about what happened?" Womack inquired.

The sheriff's face darkened considerably. "Of course I did. How are those two men doing?"

"Doc Reece is tending to them now. Looks like Dave Anderson should pull through but things are not so good for Edgar Fuller."

"That's a shame."

"It is," Womack said. He paused, perhaps waiting for the sheriff to speak again. When nothing seemed to be forthcoming from the lawman, Womack asked, "Are you intending to do anything about the attack?"

"That happened out in Fall Pass, right?"

"That's right."

The sheriff held his hands out as if he were passing something over and then pressed his palms together. "That's outside of town limits."

"Funny, because when I went to the marshal about this, he said it was a town matter."

"Well, strictly speaking, it's not something I would expect the marshal to deal with. If there was an escaped fugitive or some outlaws . . . if either of those men were ambushed by bandits . . . it would fall more in line with his regular duties." Leaning forward expectantly, the sheriff asked, "Were either of the men shot, by any chance?"

"No."

Once again, the sheriff clapped his hands together as if to prove just how empty they were. "There now. That just shows it wasn't done by any gunmen."

"A man can kill another man without using a gun," Slocum pointed out.

"Very true. From what I heard, though, those men were ripped to pieces. Mauled by some animal. The marshal's responsibilities don't extend to hunting wild game in the woods outside of town."

"What about ensuring the safety of folks who live in this town?" Slocum asked.

"That can only go so far," the sheriff said. "Regrettably we can only keep the peace within certain limitations. If a good citizen of this town were traveling, say, to Cheyenne and got robbed there . . . neither I nor the marshal could do much about it."

"Don't talk to us like we're fools," Slocum snapped. "Those two men were attacked while doing their jobs, and their jobs are at that mill, which, as I understand it, is the foundation of this damn town."

The sheriff's face took on a stern expression. "I'll thank you not to take that tone with me."

"And I'll thank you to—"

"What I believe my friend is trying to say," Womack cut in

before Slocum pushed the conversation even further in a bad direction, "is that something needs to be done about this. Whoever or whatever hurt those men is still out there."

"Man or beast," Krueger said, "it could very well have moved on by now."

"Is that the stance of the law in this town?" Slocum asked with a snide laugh. "If that's the case, remind me to rob the bank and then ride out of eyeshot."

"That's not fair, Mr. Slocum. Surely you don't expect the law of a town to bother itself with every wild animal living in the woods?"

"I would if that animal mauled two men!"

"Then perhaps you'd like to go out and hunt this beast down yourself?" Krueger said as if he was issuing a challenge that he knew wouldn't be answered.

For that reason alone, Slocum replied, "Perhaps I will! And if I catch whoever is out there, I'll expect to be paid!"

The sheriff shrugged and then nodded. "That's only fair."

"Ah!" Womack said. "That sounds like a marvelous solution."

"Wait. What just happened here?" Slocum asked.

The sheriff stood up and Womack followed suit. Reaching a hand across his desk, the lawman said, "If you're offering to lead a hunting party to find this beast, this town would be much obliged. I can send one of my boys out with you, but I don't have nearly enough men to spare for something like this. That's about all it boils down to, really. Surely you understand."

"Yeah," Slocum grunted as he turned to glare at the man standing beside him. "I understand just fine."

"Which deputy would you suggest coming along with us?" Womack asked.

After a small amount of thought, the lawman replied, "I suppose Charlie would do well enough. He's done some hunting."

"Forget it," Slocum said. "How much of a fee are we talking, Sheriff?"

"What do you mean, forget it?" the sheriff asked. "Are you interested or not?"

"I'm interested," Slocum replied. "Just not in your deputy. If he's got some real tracking experience, he might be of some use. As for hunting . . . hell, just about any man has done some hunting. If that's all your man has to offer, then he'd probably just get in the way."

"He knows these woods pretty well," the sheriff offered.

"So do the men that Mr. Womack is offering to send along with me."

When the sheriff looked over at him, Womack shrugged and nodded sheepishly. Krueger looked back to Slocum with almost complete indifference. "Fine with me if you want to go it alone," he said. "Means more men around here to keep the peace."

Slocum kept to himself all the comments that sprang to mind as far as the sheriff's ability to keep the peace.

"As far as making it worth your while," the sheriff continued, "I suppose I could pay what I'd pay any man who signed up to ride in a posse."

"Does that go for my men as well?" Womack asked. "I'm not trying to be greedy. I just know they'll ask."

"Sure. Wouldn't be good for them to know one's getting paid and the rest ain't. Any man that goes out in search of this killer, be it man or beast, will get a posse fee. Of course, since me or none of my men are going along with you, I can only pay if you bring the killer in. Otherwise, for all I know, you boys could just go out and sleep under the stars for a few nights."

Womack chuckled at that as if he and the sheriff were two old friends swapping jokes while smoking cigars on a porch. Slocum didn't even pretend to be as amused.

10

Slocum and Womack had left the sheriff's office and were half-way down Cedar Street before either of them said a word. Casually, Womack said, "I think that went pretty well, don't you?"

"About as good as I should have expected, I suppose."

"Well, at any rate, it's good that I spoke to both the lawmen. Wouldn't want to step on any toes."

Finally, Slocum cracked a smile. "Step on any toes? One of those law dogs would have had to poke more than their nose out from their offices for their toes to get stepped on."

"I can't really argue there. Are you still willing to lead the hunting party?"

"I'm leading it now?"

"Can't think of any man more qualified for the job."

"What sort of bonus does leadership come with?" Slocum asked.

"One free drink," Womack replied with a slap on Slocum's back. "What the hell. Make it two!"

Out of habit, Slocum led the way into the Axe Handle Saloon. It was the place where he'd been spending a good amount of his time when he wasn't working at the mill. On his way inside, he glanced across the street to the Second Saloon and pondered going in there to check on Eliza. But the night was young and he figured there would be plenty of time to cross the street later on.

The Axe Handle was a simple saloon that knew exactly what its patrons wanted. The bar took up most of one half of the narrow main floor, there was a stage that was just large enough for two or three scantily clad girls to kick up their heels, and the rest of the space was devoted to a few round card tables where games were played for all kinds of stakes. Already, several of the mill's workers were there gambling away their pay or handing it over to any of a number of working girls making their rounds. One of those girls spotted Slocum immediately and cut her way through the crowd to greet him.

"Well, well," she said as she strutted toward him. "If it isn't John Slocum. Here I thought you'd abandoned me for the girls across the street." She was a bit shorter than most of the women there and had curves that bordered on being too generous. Fortunately, those curves were all in the right spots to give her rounded hips and large breasts that swayed beneath the loose-fitting material of her low-cut blouse.

Never one to pass an opportunity to get his hands on a body like that, Slocum took her into his arms and gave her a playful pat on the backside. "Why the hell would I forsake you for any other, Nellie?"

Tossing her mane of strawberry blond hair over one shoulder, Nellie replied, "I can't think of a reason. Lord knows I take good care of you when you're here." She looked over at Womack and added, "I could still take care of you as well, you know."

"I know, Nellie," Womack said with a shaky nod. "But we're just here for drinks."

Winking at them, Nellie said, "That's what all the men say." She pressed herself against Slocum so her soft, plump breasts rubbed against his chest, and then she reached down to cup his groin. "I bet I can convince you to change your mind before too long."

"I bet you could," Slocum said.

Womack placed a hand upon Slocum's shoulder. "Just so you know, missy, this man was robbed recently and doesn't have much in the way of money. I'm treating him to a drink if you'd care to join us."

Nellie wriggled enticingly away from Slocum, allowing him to get a lingering feel of her breasts and hips as she stepped back. "I already drink for free in here," she said. "Sorry to hear about what happened."

"Maybe I'll tell you about it later," Slocum said.

"Maybe." With that, Nellie waved at both men and sauntered off to greener pastures.

Turning his attention to Womack, Slocum said, "Money isn't the only reason she crawls into my bed, you know. I've only decided to pay her a couple of times and she still comes back for more."

"I have no doubt about that," Womack said. "But at least I bought us some breathing room for a few minutes. Let's get them drinks."

Both of them were recognized by most everyone in the Axe Handle, but for vastly different reasons. The men who tossed waves at Womack or shared a few words with him on the way to the bar did so because they either worked for him or knew someone who did. Most of the ones who paid their respects to Slocum were either former drinking partners or had sat across from him at a poker table since he'd arrived in town. By the time they'd found a spot to stand at the bar, they'd socialized with over half the folks in the place.

"A whiskey for me and my friend," Womack said to the barkeep. "I'm buying."

"I'll take my two drinks right now," Slocum said. "Just in case you try to squirm out of your offer."

The barkeep looked over to Womack, who rolled his eyes and nodded. After the barkeep had stepped away to fetch the liquor, Womack said, "I'm a man of my word, John. You should know as much by now."

"I'm not doubting your word," Slocum replied. "I'm doubting your tolerance for whiskey. I've seen you slur your words after one beer. Can't have things slipping your mind after the first drink of red-eye."

"Fair enough," Womack sighed. "And since we're talking about reputations, I'd appreciate you not wandering off to keep company with one of these ladies before I get a chance to introduce you to the men who you'll be leading out into the woods to hunt that killer."

Just then, the barkeep returned with their drinks. He set two glasses down in front of them and poured some whiskey from a bottle with no label. Slocum lifted his glass and said, "Here's to a good hunt," before tossing the drink down. As soon as he set the glass back on the bar, it was filled with another shot of whiskey. Since Womack had had his whiskey to join Slocum in his toast, the barkeep looked over at him to see if he wanted a refill.

"Why the hell not?" Womack said good-naturedly.

The barkeep smiled and gave him another as well. "Should I leave the bottle?" he asked.

"Why the hell n—"

Cutting off Slocum's enthusiastic response, Womack said, "I may buy a round or two for the others we're meeting, but we won't need the entire bottle."

"I can just leave it for when they get here."

Looking over at Slocum, Womack said, "Why don't I let you know when we need something?"

"Suit yourself," the barkeep said before taking the bottle to some of his other thirsty customers.

"Try not to get too far along where the liquor is concerned," Womack said. "I expect you to ride out tomorrow. There's a killer out there and we can't let any grass grow beneath our feet before going after him. Or . . . it."

"I got a pretty good look at those wounds," Slocum said. "I still say it wasn't any bear."

"I agree."

"So maybe I don't know what else is out there that could do that to a man. That sure as hell wasn't the work of a wildcat unless you grow them awfully damn big around here. I'd be hard pressed to say it was even a wolf."

"That weren't no wolf," said the scrawny young fellow who approached the bar to stand beside Womack. Although he wasn't very large, he had a fierce glare that made it obvious he was willing to prove himself to anyone who decided to test him. His hair was a messy tangle of sandy brown, and his eyes were narrowed as if he were staring straight into the morning sun. Apart from a pistol strapped around his waist, he also wore the scabbard for a knife that was almost large enough to chop down a tree.

"Oh, there you are!" Womack said. "Glad you could join us. First round of drinks is on me."

When he saw Womack wave at him for the whiskey, the barkeep walked over as if every step were a burden. Slamming down a glass and filling it, he asked, "Sure you don't want me to leave the bottle?"

"Yes, I'm sure."

"It'd be easier if I left it."

"No need," Womack replied.

Muttering to himself, the barkeep shuffled away.

"John Slocum," Womack said, "this is Merle Beasley. Merle, this is John Slocum."

Merle kept one hand on the hilt of his knife while extending the other to Slocum. Even when Slocum shook his hand, Merle looked ready to draw his blade and start swinging.

"Pleased to meet you," Slocum said. "I take it you're one of the men that will be going out on the hunt?"

Merle nodded once. "Yeah, I'll be out there hunting. Can you hold your own?"

"I'd like to think so."

"You better be sure. I ain't about to be slowed down by no greenhorn who's got no damn business out in the wild. Especially considering the game we're after."

"So you don't think it's a wolf," Slocum said. "What about a bear?"

Leaning down a bit, Merle spat a juicy wad onto the floor several feet away from the closest spittoon. "I got a look at what was left of Edgar and Dave. If they were attacked by a bear, they'd be a lot worse off. Besides that, them wounds weren't put there by any claws I've ever seen."

"That's what I guessed," Slocum said. "More or less."

"I ain't guessing," Merle said while scowling as if his family name had just been insulted.

"Well then, what do you think got at those men?"

Merle took his drink, finished half of it in one gulp, and leaned against the bar so he could survey the entire room. "You must not be from around these parts."

"I'm not," Slocum replied. "What's that got to do with anything?"

After finishing his drink, Merle said, "Because if you were from around here, you would've heard about the Beast of Fall Pass."

Slocum looked over at Womack, who had no interest in looking back. "All right, then. I give up. What's the Beast of Fall Pass?"

"It's been killing men in them woods for the last few years. Before that, it was still killing but nobody wanted to admit it was anything more than a bear or a wolf."

Nudging Womack, Slocum asked, "Did you know about this?"

"I've, um, heard a thing or two."

"And why is it I haven't heard anything about it until now?"

"Because they're mostly just wild stories," Womack replied with an unconvincing shrug. "Some folks don't even think the beast is real."

"And some have seen the thing with their own two eyes," Merle said.

Slocum was always wary of local legends. More often than not, such things were a mix of superstition and ignorance. Whatever it was, however, this legend had mauled at least two men, which gave it more credence than most subjects of tall tales passed around by drunks. "And what exactly did they see?" he asked.

When Merle grinned, he flashed a set of crooked, chipped teeth stained by the tobacco he'd spat upon the floor. "You ain't told him about none of this, Mr. Womack?"

"I didn't want to bias him before he headed out to start looking. I have mentioned my belief that it could be man or beast that so grievously wounded those two men."

"Mentioning a beast is one thing," Slocum pointed out. "Failing to mention *the* Beast of Fall Pass is another."

Womack grinned and tried to laugh it off. "What's in a name, right?"

"Nothing would have a name like that unless it was something more than just a wild animal. And if that name is so common around here, it means you knew more about it than what you let on in the first place."

"Well, I didn't want anyone getting skittish. That's why I didn't mention it when I addressed my workers also."

"Nah," Slocum said with a confident shake of his head. "That's not it. You didn't want me asking for more pay for going after a known killer like this beast."

"You wouldn't do it just because it poses a threat and has so gravely wounded those men?" Womack asked.

"Sure I would," Slocum said. "And because of the added danger which you already knew would be there, the pay for this hunting expedition is going to be double what you originally offered."

Womack attempted to appear threatening when he stood up straight and asked, "Is it now?"

"Yeah," Slocum replied in a genuinely threatening manner. "It is. For any of us going out in those woods after that thing."

Merle's laugh was a dry, grating sound. "I like this fella," he said.

Reluctantly, Womack said, "Fine. I'll pay your fee."

"Don't sound so put out by it all," Slocum said. "You know well enough that you can make up that money in a dozen different ways once we bring in that beast for you. An enterprising fellow like yourself must have already thought of such things."

"Why, I don't know what you're . . ." Womack trailed off when he caught Slocum glaring at him. "All right," he said. "Maybe I have thought of a few different ways to make up my expenses once this is over."

"There you go!" Merle declared. "In fact, I'd bet you could just as easily make up the expenses of buying another round of drinks!"

Slocum grinned and raised his glass. "I think I'm starting to like this fella as well."

11

They got their free drinks, and by the time he'd had his third one, which was not on the house, Womack wasn't so cross about footing the bill. That timing was ideal, since he passed out after his fourth drink. Since he had plenty of friends at the Axe Handle and had already paid what he owed, the barkeep was happy to let him sleep it off on a cot in the back room while Slocum and Merle crossed the street to the Second Saloon.

"Darryl was supposed to be here by now," Merle said. "He could still be workin', so it's probably easier if we just go see him."

Looking at the front entrance to the saloon, Slocum asked, "He works here?"

"Yeah, but don't worry. That shouldn't interfere with our hunting trip."

"I wasn't thinking it would. Just noticing what a small world it is."

Merle wasn't interested in what was going through Slocum's mind. After kicking open the front door, all he did care about was searching the place with bleary eyes until he found the man he was after. "There he is!" he declared while staggering across the room toward the gambling tables.

Slocum followed on feet that were slightly unsteady as well.

His lack of balance reminded him of the fact that he and Merle had polished off an entire bottle of whiskey after Womack had keeled over. Neither of them was in any danger of falling on their faces, but it did take some concerted effort to walk a straight line. Fortunately, they didn't have far to go.

At the end of the room where the faro tables were, a pair of men were locked up like a couple of rams butting heads over a mate. They had their heads down and were grabbing at anything they could reach to gain an advantage over the other. One man had a full beard and a round belly. The other had bristly, unevenly cut hair and the grizzled appearance of something that had been chewed up and spat out several times. At first, the portly fellow seemed to be getting over on the other one. He used pure muscle to shove his opponent against a table, pull him back, and slam him against another. Slocum noticed that Eliza was one of the faro dealers who jumped away from their table as cards and chips were sent to the floor.

Even as he was knocked around, the grizzled man had a smile on his face. "You got a hell of a lot of steam in you, Emmett!" he said. "All this over a lousy three dollars?"

Emmett grabbed a handful of the other man's shirt and held him at arm's distance. "It ain't about the three dollars! It's the point of the—"

A chopping blow from the grizzled man's knee to Emmett's groin ended that sentence before it could be completed. Whether Emmett was a tough bastard or he was just full of liquor, he wasn't about to be put down. The other man must have recognized as much because he grabbed hold of Emmett's crotch as if he was ripping an apple from a branch and crushing it into cider.

"I think I know what yer point is," the grizzled man snarled. "I can feel it right now."

Slocum looked over to Merle and asked, "Is that Darryl?"

"The one about to tear off that fat asshole's plums?" Merle replied. "That's him, all right."

"Looks like he might be in some trouble."

"Doesn't look that way to me."

"Then you're not looking hard enough. Check those tables on the right."

Merle glanced over in that direction and his proud smile quickly faded. Although everyone at the nearby poker tables had suspended their games to watch the unscheduled floor show, three of them were separating from the rest. One wore a duster, which he flipped open so he could draw a pistol from his gun belt. Another was dressed in wrinkled trousers and a shirt that looked more like a burlap sack. He drew a knife from a scabbard behind him and started sidestepping around the table closest to him. The third man made Emmett look like a reed in comparison. His gut was so large that it almost completely flopped over the holster strapped around his ample waist.

"Darryl!" Merle shouted. "Behind you!"

Darryl turned his grizzled face around to look over his shoulder. When he turned back again, Emmett pounded a meaty fist into his chin. Smiling even wider than before he'd been hit, Darryl spat some freshly spilled blood into the other man's face and said, "You shouldn't have done that."

From there, everything went to hell.

Darryl shoved Emmett back so hard that the larger man's knees buckled against the table behind him. Although he didn't fall, Emmett was unable to do much of anything once Darryl unleashed a torrent of punches and kicks into any part of Emmett's body he could reach. Like coyotes descending from high ground, the other three that Slocum had spotted rushed forward to lend a hand. Slocum might have been content to stand back and watch the fight unfold if not for the fact that Eliza was about to be dragged into the thick of it.

She was doing a good job of keeping her eyes on Darryl and Emmett, but didn't seem to notice the man with the knife circling around toward her table. From his vantage point, Slocum could tell the man with the knife meant to get in close by approaching Darryl's blind side. Merle, on the other hand, was charging into the fray while hollering like a banshee.

Rather than try to circle around or make any other sort of subtle move, Slocum took a page from Merle's book and ran at the problem head-on. After a few heavy steps, Slocum had covered almost half the distance between himself and Eliza. He was in the process of drawing the .44 Remington at his side when the man with the knife looked directly at him. For a moment, Slocum thought he might have done enough to frighten him away from Eliza's table. That moment passed when the man pivoted to snap his wrist and send his blade spinning through the air.

Slocum leaned back and turned to one side as the blade sailed so closely to his head that he could hear it singing to him when it passed. He could see the man who'd tossed the knife drawing another from his boot with one hand and reaching for Eliza with the other.

"Don't touch her!" Slocum shouted.

The man with the knife smirked, grabbed Eliza by the back of her collar, and pulled her in close to discourage Slocum from taking a shot at him. If he'd had another moment or two to aim and hadn't been in the process of running, Slocum might have been able to pick the other man off. As it was, he would be lucky if he merely wounded Eliza instead of killing her outright. Before Slocum had a chance to swear under his breath, the man threw the boot knife at him.

This time, Slocum was watching closely enough to gauge the other man's movements. The blade hadn't even made one complete end-over-end turn when he reached out with his left hand to snatch it from the air. Slocum was more surprised than anyone when he not only grabbed the knife, but wrapped his fingers around the handle instead of its blade. Still running at full speed, he lowered his shoulder to knock both the man and Eliza back.

Eliza let out a surprised yelp as she was shoved to one side.

Slocum took the man with him to the floor, shattering a wooden chair along the way. As soon as he had a chance, Slocum rolled toward the other man and drove an elbow into his chest. Since the man refused to stay down, Slocum returned the knife he'd plucked from the air by stabbing it into the other man's shoulder.

"Men like you can never do anything the easy way," Slocum growled.

The man with the knife was winded, battered, and stunned from the sharp pain coursing through his fresh wound. After knocking him out with one last punch, Slocum pulled himself to his feet.

"John!" Eliza said breathlessly. "What are you doing here?"

"Just out for a friendly drink," he replied. "You'd best find a safer place to be."

She placed a hand to her chest as if to steady her racing heart as she moved away from her table and went to the bar.

The other two men who'd intended on flanking Darryl had their hands full with Merle. The fat fellow had taken a couple of lumps already and was slumped against a poker table trying to catch his breath while the man in the duster fought for his life. Merle swung his fists like a wild man, even as he absorbed some punches of his own. Now that he'd collected himself, the fat man raised a pistol he clutched in one hand.

"Enough!" Rolf shouted from behind the bar. When nobody paid him any mind, he brought up a shotgun from where it had been stashed and fired a barrel over his head. The men involved in the fracas were still too busy defending themselves to stop now.

Slocum turned toward the bar and shouted to Rolf, "Toss me that shotgun!"

The bartender wasn't about to do any such thing until Eliza convinced him otherwise with a few sharp words. Finally, Rolf tossed his weapon toward Slocum and backed away.

Slocum grabbed the shotgun and ran across the saloon. Darryl and Emmett were still fighting tooth and nail, but Darryl was considerably less bloody than his opponent. Since Merle was outnumbered and about to be shot, Slocum set his sights on that section of the room.

"Hey, fat man!" Slocum shouted.

The portly fellow turned toward him and immediately shifted his aim when he saw the shotgun in Slocum's hands. Kicking over a chair rather than waste precious time in walking around it, Slocum got to within a few paces of the fat gunman before taking aim and pulling the shotgun's second trigger. The weapon roared in his hands and the fat man reeled, upending the table he'd been leaning against before dropping to the floor.

"Jesus Christ!" gasped the man scuffling with Merle. Having been distracted by the shotgun blast that had dropped his rotund partner, he left himself wide open.

Merle wasn't about to let an opportunity like that pass him by, so he delivered a punch to the jaw with everything he had behind it. The man's head snapped to one side and he spun partway around before staggering back and falling into the lap of a nearby gambler who'd been caught in the middle of the fight. More concerned with guarding his chips, he shoved the man to the floor and dusted off his suit.

Darryl and Emmett stood in front of each other, both gasping for air and covered in blood.

"Well now," Darryl said. "Ain't this production a bit much for three dollars?"

"I told you already," Emmett replied. "It ain't the money. It's the point that I was cheated."

"Oh! You were cheated?" Darryl proclaimed. "Well, why didn't you say so?"

Emmett was about to speak on his own behalf when Darryl drove a fist into his gut and shoved him into the waiting arms of the two young men Rolf had sent over. After spitting some blood onto the floor, Darryl looked at the two young men and asked, "Well, where the hell were you two?"

One of the young men pushed Emmett toward the door while the other replied, "You told us not to get in your way whenever you had to knock some sense into someone."

Screwing his face up as if purposely trying to look uglier, Darryl smiled and grunted, "Yeah. I suppose I did." Then he shifted his attention to Merle and asked, "Who'd you bring with you?"

"This here is John Slocum," Merle said.

"John Slocum. I heard that name before."

"He's supposed to be some sort of gunman. The boss from the mill has been going on about him like he was the second coming."

"Nah, that ain't it." After a few moments of deliberation, Darryl snapped his fingers. "I know! You're the one that's been puttin' it to that whore across the street on a regular basis! Nellie, I believe her name is."

Slocum shrugged. "I wouldn't say it's worth gossiping about, but I've been paying her a visit from time to time."

"Well, you know how the hens like to gossip. A few of the girls around here were talking about you. Of course," Darryl added, "that was when Lester Quint was coming in here trying to pass himself off as someone else."

"You knew it was Lester?" Slocum asked. "Why the hell would you let him get away with that?"

Darryl merely shrugged. "His money spends just as well one way or another. He can call himself Abraham Lincoln just so long as he keeps spendin'. Personally, I thought it was a hoot to watch him strut about the way he was."

"He's not strutting anymore," Slocum said.

Darryl slapped him on the shoulder. "And it would have been a hoot to watch someone slap Lester down. Considering what a cold-blooded killer you are, I suppose ol' Lester should be glad he's still walkin' and talkin'."

Slocum didn't care for the familiar way Darryl treated him and he liked the accusation even less. Looking down at the dirty hand that was still on his shoulder, he asked, "Cold-blooded killer? What's that supposed to mean?"

"I mean what you did to the fat man over there. You walked up and shotgunned him into next week without so much as a tip of yer damn hat!"

Looking over at the spot where the fat man in question had wound up, Slocum watched as the rotund fellow pulled himself upright, groaned, and pressed both hands flat against his chest. The man's blubbery face contorted in pain when he touched the little bloody spots that had formed on his shirt, but was able to make his way over to a chair and sit down. Slocum then looked back to Darryl and said, "That shotgun was loaded with rock salt."

"Rock salt?" Darryl then looked over at the fat man. The

glee that had been etched onto his face a moment ago was replaced by confusion and a hint of disappointment. "Huh. I suppose it was. How the hell did you know that?"

"That barkeep fired one barrel into the ceiling and barely did any damage," Slocum replied. "I figured the other barrel was loaded with the same kind of shot and put it to use."

"And what if it hadn't been loaded the same?"

"Then that fat man over there would've had a very bad night."

Darryl found his gleeful expression again and marked its reappearance with another slap to Slocum's back. "He sure would have! And I would've had to clean the damn mess! Ha!" Looking at Merle, he said, "Where the hell did you find this one, little brother?"

"The three of us were offered a job," Merle said.

"What kind of job?"

"Huntin' out in the woods outside of town."

"Sounds better than working in this rat trap," Darryl replied. "Huntin' usually don't pay as well as what I'm makin' here or you're makin' at the mill."

"Depends on what we're huntin'."

Finally, Darryl shifted his aggressive attentions to someone other than Slocum. Making Merle seem even skinnier by comparison, Darryl wrapped a thick arm around his neck and shook him while saying, "This one always did like dragging things out. What's the damn job, Merle?"

Although Merle tried to speak, he couldn't get much out due to the arm around his neck and the way he was being tossed back and forth. While the brothers wrestled, Rolf and a few of the other saloon workers emerged from where they'd been hiding to clean up the mess that had been made.

Before long, Merle disentangled himself and sent a few quick jabs to Darryl's ribs. The older of the two grunted, held his hands palms out, and encouraged his brother to keep fighting. "What are we gonna kill, Merle? Tell me before I get rough."

"We're goin' after the beast."

"Which beast?"

Slapping away his brother's paw-like hands, Merle dropped

his voice to a grating whisper and said, "The Beast of Fall Pass. Didn't you hear about the two men that were mauled?"

"I ain't heard much," Darryl said. "I been workin' here or drunk. Or both. You serious about this?"

"Mr. Womack at the mill is serious and he's the one payin' us to bring back that thing's hide."

"Well, all right, then!" Darryl hollered.

Slocum shook his head and made his way to the front door. "Christ," he grumbled under his breath. "What the hell have I signed up for?"

12

Slocum made his way to the Morrison House and nearly collapsed when he got there. All was quiet inside the place. Helga was in her room, asleep or otherwise. All Slocum really cared about was that the old woman didn't pounce on him the moment he stepped through the front door. There was one lantern giving off a bit of light. It was turned down so only a barely glowing flame was burning, and Slocum twisted the knob to put it all the way out before finding his way to the stairs. Instead of going to his room once he'd climbed to the second floor, he shuffled down the hall to the last door on the left and knocked.

Before his knuckles had finished tapping, the door was pulled open and Greta peeked out through the crack. Almost immediately, she opened the door the rest of the way. She wore a long white nightgown with a lace collar and flowing sleeves. Even though the garment was loose on her, the material was thin enough to show her pert breasts behind the fabric.

"There you are, John," she whispered. "I was starting to worry."

Slocum was about to speak, but was pulled inside so the door could be shut. Greta pressed herself against him and kissed him hard on the mouth. It didn't take long at all for

Slocum to respond by reaching around to feel her tight little ass. He tasted her lips and his cock grew hard as cast iron to strain against his jeans.

Grinding her hips against him, Greta said, "I see you've been just as anxious as I have."

"This is gonna be my last night here for a while. Figured I'd make the best of it."

Greta pulled her face back so she could get a better look at him. "Are you being serious?"

"Afraid so."

"Where are you going?"

"I'll be riding out in the morning," Slocum told her. "Going hunting in the woods for a spell."

"How long will you be gone?"

"As long as it takes," he replied while moving his hands around to feel the slope of her lower back and the upper swell of her buttocks.

"When were you going to tell me?" she pouted.

Slocum licked the base of her neck and chewed on her earlobe before saying, "I'm telling you right now. I only just found out myself."

Stepping away from him, Greta backed toward the bed. Her room was a bit smaller than the one Slocum had been renting, which meant there was just enough room for the two of them, a good-sized bed, a dresser, and a wardrobe. "So, you only came knocking on my door to have a warm bed to sleep in before you have only your horse to keep you company?"

"I've got a warm bed in my room," Slocum replied as he stalked after her. "I came looking for something . . . warmer."

"Maybe I do not like being how you pass the time before you leave."

If not for the mischievous smirk on her face, which was barely visible in the dim light of her lantern, Slocum might have believed she was serious. Even if she hadn't been teasing him, he still would have stepped right up to her and grabbed her around the waist to draw her in. "You've been after me since I got here," he said.

"I wouldn't have been after you if you did not come after me first."

"Well, here I am again."

"And maybe I would rather sleep on my own tonight."

"We'll just see about that." Having already backed Greta against the edge of her bed, Slocum gave her a gentle push, which sent her straight down to the mattress. She landed with a surprised yelp, which she quickly suppressed.

"You'll wake my mother," she hissed.

Slocum unbuckled his gun belt and set it on the dresser. "Then you'd best not make any noise."

"What are you doing?" she asked as Slocum unbuttoned his shirt and gazed down at her.

His only response was a devilish grin. Next, he reached down for her legs and slid his hands up to push her nightgown up toward her waist.

"Oh, no you don't," she giggled. "I should be cross at you."

"Maybe you should," Slocum admitted. "That's why I intend on making it up to you."

"How could you do that?"

Instead of telling her, Slocum pushed her nightgown up past her hips to expose Greta's milky thighs and the curly patch of hair between them. After tossing his hat away, he spread her legs open wide and pressed his mouth against her pussy. The suddenness of his move took her breath away and she arched her back while grabbing the back of his head with both hands. As Slocum's tongue ran along the lips of her pussy, she lifted her backside off the bed to rub herself against his face.

Slocum cupped her ass in both hands and probed her with his tongue. She was already damp when he started, and after only a few seconds, she was dripping. Greta's straining breaths filled the room and she fought to keep from crying out when his mouth found her clit. Lingering on the sensitive nub of flesh, he teased her until he felt her body tense. Then he flicked the tip of his tongue on her with renewed intensity.

Greta's entire body started to shake. Her fingers clamped around Slocum's head, holding him in place as her heels dug into his back just below his shoulders. She turned her head to one side and spread her legs open as wide as they could go, savoring every second of the climax that hit her like a storm. Even after she'd stopped trembling, she held Slocum's head in place. He licked her a bit more, moving his tongue along the inside of her thighs, up her flat stomach, and between her heaving breasts. Her skin was warm and sweaty beneath the nightgown, and she was more than happy to wriggle out of the loose-fitting garment.

"So," Slocum said as he straightened up to rise above her. "You still angry with me coming in here this way?"

"You . . ." she gasped while tugging at the front of his jeans to try and pull them off him. "You're forgiven."

Slocum stood and removed his shirt as she tore his jeans off and knelt in front of him so she could suck his rigid pole. Her head bobbed back and forth, devouring every inch of his erection as her hands wandered up his bare chest and down along his sides. Slocum had hoped he could get her going, but even he was taken aback by how eagerly she attacked him. He wasn't about to complain, however, and closed his eyes while her lips and tongue slid along his shaft.

Reaching down to hold her face in his hands, Slocum eased her back. She looked up at him, licked her lips, and asked, "You don't like what I do?"

For some reason, Greta's European accent grew thicker when she was aroused. Whether it was genuine or some way to purposely entice him, it worked like a charm.

"I like it just fine," he assured her. "But I want more."

"More?" she asked while coyly batting her eyelashes. "What could be more than that?" She was definitely playing with him now, but was doing a good enough job that he didn't mind one bit.

He picked her up and threw her naked on the bed in front of him. Rolling onto her side, Greta writhed on the blanket as if her orgasm was still tickling different parts of her body. By the time Slocum had stripped bare, she was on all fours with her chest rubbing against the bed and her backside lifted in the

air toward him to create a beautiful slope that ran all the way
down her back to the nape of her neck.

Greta grabbed on to the edge of her mattress and
moaned softly into her blanket as Slocum buried his cock
between her legs. She was so wet that he glided in and out of
her with ease. Grabbing her hips with both hands, he pumped
into her vigorously. When he drove every inch of his erection
home, Greta tossed her hair back and let out a long, trembling
breath.

Allowing his instincts to dictate his actions, Slocum grabbed
some of her hair in his right hand and placed his left upon the
small of her back. Sliding out of her, he thrust back in while
giving her hair a tug.

"Oh yes," she softly moaned. "More. Like that."

Slocum pumped into her with a slow, pounding rhythm.
When he buried his cock all the way in again, he kept it there
and ground his hips against her backside. He pulled her hair a
little harder until she leaned back as far as she could while
trembling in anticipation. Before he hurt her, Slocum let go of
her hair and reached around to cup Greta's tits in both hands
while pumping into her again.

"I . . . want to ride you," she breathed. "Right now."

Never one to refuse a lady, Slocum eased out of her so he
could lie down on her bed and she could straddle his hips.
Greta's body was breathtaking in the flickering light from the
room's single lantern. Her hips were small but rounded, as were
her breasts. He reached up to cup them and felt her small nipples stiffen immediately against his palms. For a few moments,
she simply sat astride him with her eyes closed, savoring the
way he touched her. Slocum moved his hands along the front
of his body before reaching down her stomach to rub small
circles on her clit with his thumb.

Greta's eyes snapped open and her mouth curled into a wide
smile. "You're going to make me—" Before she could finish
her sentence, she was overpowered by another climax. Slocum
was amazed at how much she trembled at his touch. It was as
if she'd been drawn tighter than a bowstring while waiting for

him that night, which made Slocum feel foolish for making her wait so long.

She was still panting breathlessly when she reached down to guide his cock between her legs. The moment she felt his rigid member slip inside her once more, she let out a satisfied grunt. From then on, Greta rode him with reckless abandon. Her fingers raked against Slocum's chest as she rocked back and forth on top of him. Taking every inch inside, she leaned her head back and pumped her hips in a furious rhythm as sweat rolled down her pert breasts and erect nipples. All Slocum had to do was lie back and enjoy the show. And it was one hell of a fine show.

When her passion reached yet another peak, she lowered herself so her hands were flat against the bed on either side of Slocum's head and her face was less than an inch away from his. He wrapped both arms around her, placing one hand on her backside and sliding the fingers of his other hand through her long blond hair. While holding her tightly that way, he pumped up into her.

Greta's entire body trembled. He could tell by the way she breathed into his ear that she was awfully close to crying out loud. Slocum wanted to drive her over that edge just to prove he could and just to hear what Greta sounded like when she truly cut loose. So far, every time they'd been together, she'd reined herself in and asked him to do the same so as not to alert her mother. Slocum didn't feel compelled to appease the old woman, but he did respect Greta's wishes.

Suddenly, she straightened her arms to rise slightly above him. Her head turned to one side and her expression reflected the intensity of what she was feeling. Her hips moved with an insistent pace that drove Slocum to his own precipice. Watching her ride him as sweat trickled down the front of her naked body, Slocum was taken to the point of no return and exploded inside her. When his tremors had subsided, Greta opened her eyes and smiled down at him.

"That was nice," she whispered.

"Yes," Slocum replied breathlessly. "It sure was."

She climbed off him so she could lie beside him and drape an arm and leg across Slocum's body. One of his legs hung over the side of the mattress, but he was too exhausted to do much about it.

They stayed there for a while, drifting in and out of sleep. Just as Slocum was wondering if she was awake, he heard her voice in the near-darkness.

"Where are you going tomorrow?" she asked.

"Hunting."

"Hunting for what?"

"Some animal mauled a couple of workers from the mill," he told her. "Did you hear anything about that?"

"I heard about some men getting hurt, but I didn't think too much of it. Men often get hurt while working around those big saws and machinery."

"Those men weren't hurt by any saws."

Greta propped herself up on one elbow so she could look at him while lying on her side. "What happened to them?"

"They were attacked by something. Or . . . someone. We're not really sure. Well," Slocum added, "some think they're sure."

The confusion on Greta's face was understandable, since it was also somewhat reflected on Slocum's. "I don't understand," she said.

Rolling onto his side so he could look directly into her eyes, Slocum asked, "Have you ever heard of the Beast of Fall Pass?"

The confusion left her face, only to be replaced by something else. Something darker. "I have heard people talk about that. My mother would know more of it than I would."

"Your mother?"

She nodded. "When people here started talking about that beast, my mother told me about creatures that roamed the woods where she grew up in Germany." Greta shuddered. "They were terrible stories."

"What were the stories?" When he saw how rattled she was, Slocum gently moved some of the hair from where it had fallen in front of her face and said, "They can't be that bad. Probably just stories meant to frighten children."

"She . . . spoke of men that would turn into wolves. Men who'd been cursed. Women, too. When they . . . changed . . . they would eat children. They would tear people apart limb from limb."

Slocum couldn't help laughing just a little. He didn't want to be rude, but he couldn't exactly hide it either.

Greta gave him a little shove and rolled onto her other side so her back was to him. "Don't laugh at me."

"I'm not laughing at you."

"Yes, you are. I heard you."

"Not laughing at you exactly," Slocum insisted. "Just . . . that story is kind of . . ." He searched for words to use that would relay what he was thinking without offending her any further and settled for the least offensive of the bunch. "It's kind of far-fetched. Don't you think?"

Although he couldn't see her face, her smooth shoulder moved in a shrug. "I suppose," she said. "But that is what she told me."

"Is that what people are saying about the Beast of Fall Pass?"

"Not exactly."

"Tell me what they're saying. Please."

"Why?" she scoffed. "Are you hunting the Beast of Fall Pass?"

After a few seconds of silence, Slocum replied, "That's what some are saying attacked those men I told you about."

Greta rolled back around so quickly that some of her hair whipped Slocum across the cheek. She stared at him intently and asked, "Are you joking with me after what I told you about my mother's stories?"

"Wish I was, but the men paying me to go into those woods are dead serious and those men that were hurt . . . well . . . at least one of them may be just plain dead by now."

"They were ripped limb from limb?"

"Wasn't quite that bad, but pretty damn close," Slocum said. "Looked like it was an animal that did the job, but the more I've been thinking about it, the less certain I am."

"Why do you say that?"

"Something about the wounds themselves that . . ." When he paid closer attention to Greta's face instead of losing himself in his own thoughts, Slocum could see that she was still plenty rattled. Rather than dwelling on the gruesome details, he said, "Whatever it is truly doesn't matter, I suppose, since we'll be heading out after it one way or another."

"Who is going with you?"

"Merle and Darryl Beasley." Even in the dim light, Slocum could see the disgust on Greta's face. "You've heard of them?"

"They came to town around the same time my mother opened this boardinghouse. They needed a place to stay and rented some rooms here. One night, the younger brother tried to have his way with me, and the next night, the older one tried as well."

"Did they force themselves on you?" he asked in a tense voice.

"No, but they were both very insistent. They said they wanted to do things to me, but they didn't touch me. They are pigs."

"No argument there. I've already met them. You're sure they didn't lay a hand on you?"

"I am sure," she said with a shudder. "I wouldn't forget a thing like that." She blinked a few times before truly taking notice of the fire that was smoldering in Slocum's eyes. In a much lighter tone, she added while rubbing the side of his face, "They did nothing but say disgusting words to me."

"If it was more than that, I might have to rip them apart worse than any beast could."

"If they did more than that, I would want to watch while you did that to them."

Satisfied, Slocum felt his anger subside. "Those two may be pigs, but they're supposed to know these woods pretty well. We're to ride out to where those men were attacked and track whatever it was that spilled their blood. Once we find it, we'll know for certain whether it's man or beast. The only reason I asked you about it was because anything you could tell me about what I'm supposed to be going after might be of some use."

Greta chewed on her lower lip while taking some time to think. As she pondered her next words, she idly played with a few strands of her hair. Considering the fact that she was still naked and glistening with sweat from their lovemaking, it was quite a sight to behold. She gave him another pretty sight when she sat upright without bothering to cover herself. "I just remembered something!"

"I'm listening," Slocum replied, even though his eyes were lingering on the tight contours of her bare flesh.

"There were some trappers that stayed here last year and they said they saw the Beast of Fall Pass."

"Did they really?"

Reaching out, Greta placed her finger beneath Slocum's chin and raised his head so he was looking at her face instead of several inches lower. "Do you want to hear this or not?"

"I want plenty of things."

"First of all, they said the beast was large."

"No surprise there," Slocum said. "Even if an animal is no bigger than a dog, folks will say it's a giant so they don't look like pansies for fearing it."

"They didn't say it was tall, but . . ." Greta sat up straight, puffed out her cheeks and held her arms out to mimic someone three times heavier than she. "Large. Like this."

"Oh. I see." Slocum reached out to slide his hand along her leg all the way up to her hip. "Was that all?"

"No. They also said it made a strange sound. Like heavy breaths or wheezing."

Slocum's hand stopped midway between her knee and hip. "They said it was wheezing?"

"Yes."

"That's a bit strange."

"Not as strange as the smell," Greta said. "They said it smelled terribly bad. Like rotten meat and garbage."

"Rotten meat and . . . garbage?"

"Yes. The men were speaking to my mother about the beast and that is what they said."

"What did your mother have to say about that?"

"She said the wolves from Germany smelled only like wolves and blood. Such gruesome stories."

It may have been gruesome, but it resonated in Slocum's mind. If Helga had claimed all monsters smelled like that, it could have just been some common bit of folklore that was passed around. But since that piece only came from the men who claimed to have seen the Beast of Fall Pass, that meant it might be something he could actually use. "What happened with those men who saw the beast? Did they try to hunt it? Was one of them hurt?"

"No. They were only frightened after seeing it in the woods. They and my mother talked for hours about such things. Most of it was just stories, but those things I told you were what they said when they first started talking and were still frightened. The rest," Greta said with a casual flick of her hand, "was just stories told around the fire."

"That was helpful."

"You are joking with me again?"

"Not hardly," Slocum said. "Is there anything else you can tell me?"

She smiled and pushed Slocum so he was lying flat on his back. Her hand slipped between his legs and she started stroking him as she said, "I am through with talking."

"What if I'm not?" Slocum asked. Even though his mind was wandering in other directions as well, he liked the way Greta was trying to convince him to end the conversation.

She smiled and accepted the challenge he'd thrown down by moving her head between his legs and wrapping her lips around his cock. Her tongue slid along the bottom of his pole and she sucked on him greedily.

Slocum leaned back and grew harder in her mouth. He was definitely through with talking as well.

13

Considering how much Darryl had drunk the night before and the state he was in the next morning, Slocum was amazed the grizzled man was able to sit upright in his saddle. The sun was still low on the eastern horizon as they took the trail out of town that led into the surrounding woods. Merle rode out front with Darryl behind and Slocum bringing up the rear. Apart from a few grunted greetings when they'd first met up, not many words had passed between any of them that entire morning.

"You all right up there, Darryl?" Slocum finally asked.

Darryl was slouched forward and had begun to lean a bit too far to the right. Rather than center himself on the saddle, he waved off Slocum's question and grumbled something in a slurred voice.

"He's fine," Merle said. "Just needs to let all that whiskey burn out of his belly." Turning in his saddle, the younger brother shouted, "Ain't that right, Darryl?"

Swinging at the air as if Merle's raised voice were a swarm of bees stinging his ears, Darryl grunted some more. This time, however, several obscene comments could distinctly be heard.

"He's in rough shape," Slocum pointed out. "If he doesn't get right soon, he'll just be slowing us down."

Merle shifted back around to face front. "We're headed to a spot we know. Once we get there, we'll water the horses and let Darryl mix up a batch of his tonic. After that, he'll be right as rain."

"You sure about that?"

"For the love of God," Darryl bellowed, "will the both of you shut yer goddamn holes? My head's fixin' to crack in two."

When Merle turned around again, he wore a smile that was twice as wide as it had been the last time. "Whose fault is that, you damn fool?"

"Whoever brewed that damn whiskey! Now shut the hell up," Darryl snarled as he drew the .45-caliber Colt strapped to his hip, "before I drill a hole through your yappin' skull!"

Merle chuckled as if he were being threatened by a cork gun. "You won't pull that trigger."

"Why the hell not? 'Cause you're my brother? We been kin long enough for the appeal to wear mighty thin."

"Nah," Merle replied. "Because pulling that trigger would make too much noise."

Darryl was sighting along the top of his barrel at a point somewhere between his brother's shoulder blades. As he'd watched the two men squabble, Slocum put his hand on the grip of his holstered Remington. Although he wasn't particularly fond of either brother, he wasn't about to let one of them shoot the other in an act of drunken stupidity. When Darryl turned around to fix a hazy stare on him, Slocum tensed his arm in preparation to put the Remington to work.

"You know somethin'?" Darryl slurred. "I think he's got a point." Then he started laughing while pointing his gun skyward and easing the hammer down with his thumb.

Whether or not Merle knew that his brother's pistol had been cocked and ready to fire, he merely shook his head and laughed while flicking his reins to keep his horse moving down the trail.

It took several attempts, but Darryl eventually found his holster well enough to slide his pistol back into it. After he'd put the gun away, he held on to his reins with both hands and slouched to one side just as he'd been when they'd first left town.

"Jesus H. Christ," Slocum grumbled. He allowed his hand to move away from the Remington, but wouldn't fully relax as long as either of the Beasley brothers were in his sight.

Just ahead, the trail split off with one branch leading north and the other northeast. Darryl gave his reins a tug to steer his horse down the former.

"Hey!" Slocum shouted. Despite the angry glare he got from Darryl, he didn't bother lowering his voice when he asked, "Isn't Fall Pass to the northeast?"

"Yeah," Merle shouted back. "So?"

"So . . . that's where we're headed."

"Not yet. We gotta make a stop first."

"What stop?" Slocum waited for an answer, but none was forthcoming. He didn't fool himself into thinking that either brother had much respect for authority, but Slocum had another intention when he said, "Womack put me in charge of this ride, you know."

Merle brought his horse to a stop so quickly that Darryl's nearly bumped into its hind end, which was the exact thing Slocum had expected to happen. "Womack ain't here, in case you hadn't noticed."

Now that he had both men's undivided attention, Slocum rode closer to the front of the line. He wasn't stupid enough, however, to go so far as to put Darryl behind him. "At the very least, we're in this together. You mind telling me why we're not headed in the right direction?"

"Me and Darryl have done plenty of hunting out in these woods," Merle said. "We got us a little spot I mentioned staked out not too far along this here trail. We're going there to pick up some supplies and then we'll mosey on over to Fall Pass. That answer your question?"

"Yeah. That wasn't so difficult, now was it?"

"Remind me again why the hell you're along on this hunt," Darryl said.

"Because I've tracked plenty of men through every kind of terrain," Slocum replied.

"If what we're goin' after ain't no man, then hunters know plenty about how to conduct themselves," Merle said.

"That's another reason it's good to have me along," Slocum said. "I'm a fresh set of eyes. Folks around here are so scared of this so-called beast that they aren't seeing straight. When you're tracking, you need to look at what you can see, not what you expect to see."

"You hear that, little brother?" Darryl said. "Johnny boy here is gonna teach us how to track!"

"You want to know the biggest reason I think Womack is glad to have me out here hunting this thing down?" Slocum asked.

"I imagine you're dyin' to tell us," Darryl said while rubbing his forehead.

"It's because I didn't show any fear when someone mentioned the Beast of Fall Pass."

"You think you can handle yourself well enough to stay alive out here?" Darryl grunted.

In a flicker of motion, Slocum drew his Remington and fired a shot that hissed through the air past both brothers to hit a squirrel that had been scampering across the trail in front of Merle's horse.

"That was a hell of a shot," Darryl admitted. "You realize the game we're after ain't no squirrel, right?"

Slocum holstered his pistol and shook his head. "Get stuffed, you drunk son of a bitch."

Darryl and Merle broke into hearty laughter. Before long, Slocum laughed as well and the entire procession made their way down the trail once again. The tension between them lifted like a bank of fog that had been burned off by the morning sun, and the three of them seemed more like a single group focused on a common task.

It wasn't long before Merle diverted once again from the trail they were riding. He steered his horse into what at first seemed to be just another cluster of bushes alongside the beaten path. Darryl followed him without a complaint and Slocum did the same. After his horse had shoved through the brush, Slocum found himself in a small clearing that was just big enough for the trio to gather around a half-buried log.

"About damn time," Darryl grunted as he climbed down from his horse. "Thought we'd never get here."

Slocum remained in his saddle as Merle dismounted. "This is the spot you were after?" he asked. "I figured it would be a cabin of some sort."

"We never said anything about no cabin," Darryl grunted.

"So where are all of your supplies?"

When Merle wandered into the brush, Slocum figured it was to relieve himself. The younger brother returned, dragging a filthy old trunk along with him. Once he'd brought the trunk into the clearing, Merle turned his back to the other two and proceeded to relieve himself.

"While he's watering the weeds," Darryl said, "I'm gonna show you the proper cure for what ails a man after a night of drinkin'."

Slocum looked around and all he could see was the clearing, the log, and a whole mess of bushes on all sides. "Didn't you mention something about watering the horses?"

Merle looked over his shoulder while continuing to piss. "There's a stream off that way. Why don't you take our horses, too, if you're goin'?"

Before he could tell the brothers to take their own damn horses to the stream, Slocum caught a whiff of something that was bitter, pungent, and spicy at the same time. Although he suspected it might have been Merle causing that stench, he realized the odor was growing stronger the more Darryl rooted around inside the trunk.

"Here we are!" Darryl said as he proudly held up a mason jar filled with a murky, dark red liquid. When he shook it and removed the top, the stench that had caught Slocum's attention became almost unbearable.

"I think I'll water those horses after all," Slocum said. He knew better than to expect any gratitude from the brothers and didn't receive any as he collected the reins to each horse and led them through the brush.

After several more steps, Slocum heard the trickle of water flowing over rocks. He followed it to its source, which was a narrow, winding stream with a clearing just wide enough for the horses to stand on the opposite side. Slocum led the horses across and then tethered them to a gnarled stump with markings that told him it had most likely been used for that same purpose over the course of several years.

All three horses were grateful for the chance to stand still for a while and wet their tongues in the cool stream. Slocum even hunkered down to dip his hand into the clear water and scoop some into his mouth. The crisp drink, partnered with the fact that he was away from the Beasley brothers, made it the best part of his day so far. He allowed his hand to dangle into the water and his eyes to focus on the slowly swaying branches on the other side of the stream while savoring the taste of the water flowing over his lips.

In the distance, the sounds of Merle and Darryl arguing about something or other drifted through the air.

Slocum closed his eyes so he could focus only on the stream.

Heavy steps pressed against the matted leaves and fallen branches covering the ground along the path Slocum had taken from the clearing. He was in the middle of trying to pin down which brother was stomping toward the stream when he heard both of their voices in the distance. Too distant, in fact, for either of them to be approaching the stream.

Slocum's eyes snapped up toward the spot where he and the horses had emerged from the bushes. His hand dropped to his holster while his entire body tensed for movement.

The footsteps stopped immediately and a heavy silence filled the air.

Water rushed down the stream.

Horses lapped up their drinks.

One more step crunched against the ground, followed by the rustle of branches and leaves scraping against each other.

Slocum forced himself to remain still even as his entire body screamed for him to draw his pistol and see what was approaching the stream. Then a rank stench hit Slocum's nose. It wasn't the mixture in Darryl's mason jar, but something even more pungent that reminded him of a dead animal that had been left in the sun to fester.

A shape emerged from behind some of the trees on the other side of the stream. It was broad and thick, but not very tall.

Thinking back to everything Greta had told him about the Beast's calling cards, Slocum drew his Remington. He considered taking a shot at whatever it was, but Slocum could still only make out a rough shape in the shadows between the trees. And as soon as he saw more than that, it was too late for him to anything but watch it bolt into the woods.

"Damn it!" Slocum growled to himself as he took off after the shape that had already disappeared from sight.

Crossing the stream, Slocum was careful not to slip and break his back. The rocks near the edges were slimy, but the silt and gravel along the center of the winding ribbon of water granted him somewhat better footing. As soon as he was able, Slocum hopped onto dry ground, where the dirt and bushes could soak up some of the water from his boots. The instant he felt he had traction again, he took off running into the trees.

With all the swaying branches and falling leaves obscuring his vision, Slocum had to rely more on what he could hear to follow the thing he'd seen. For that same reason, he didn't think to shout for Merle or Darryl to come and help him in his pursuit. All he had to go on was the steady crunch of feet against the uneven ground and the sound of heavy, labored breathing coming from several paces in front of him. Every now and then, one of those breaths was accompanied by a short, grating wheeze.

Soon, Slocum heard other footsteps closing in on him from the left. Since that was the general direction of Merle's clearing, he figured at least one of the brothers had picked up on the fact that something was going on and was trying to get close enough to lend a hand. The thing in front of him must have heard those footsteps as well because it veered to the right and deeper into the woods. Slocum jumped off the narrow path he and the horses had used in an attempt to gain some ground.

"What the hell you runnin' after?" Merle shouted from behind Slocum.

Without breaking stride, Slocum said, "There's something out here. It might be the beast!"

"Hot damn! I knew this job would be easy!"

"Don't celebrate . . ." Pausing so he could duck beneath some low branches and also keep from wrenching his ankle in some exposed roots, Slocum waited until he could take a few safe steps before saying, "Don't celebrate yet. Just help me catch the damn thing!"

Now that his ears had adjusted to the sound of all the rustling and stomping, Slocum had an easier time picking out the sounds of whatever was running in front of him. Those steps seemed irregular at first, but a pattern soon developed like the thump of drums in a simple rhythm.

A faster set of steps closed in from behind and to one side. Slocum knew that was Merle coming around to try and close in on their mutual prey. Being the youngest of the three hunters, he was also the quickest and he soon rushed past Slocum.

When he heard the heavier steps in front of them come to a stop, Slocum dug his feet into the dirt and shouted, "Hold up!"

Merle kept going at full speed while Slocum drew his pistol and moved with a bit more caution.

"Gotchya, you son of a—" Merle's words were cut short by a loud snarl and the distinctive snap of branches.

Swearing under his breath, Slocum quickened his pace and kept his eyes open for any sign of a threat. The first thing to catch his attention was a stench that grew so strong he almost gagged on it. When he saw some motion in the corner of his eye, Slocum pivoted toward it while bringing up his gun. He saw something large and shaggy a split second before getting walloped in the chest. The impact hit him solidly, forcing the air from his lungs and causing his finger to tighten around his trigger. The Remington sent its round into the dirt as Slocum dropped.

Since he'd been knocked straight back, Slocum was unable to see much of anything at first. Part of that was because his hat had been dislodged to slide halfway over his eyes. He was pushing his hat back into place when he heard footsteps coming straight at him. Slocum's gun hand came up to take aim at his attacker before he was hit again. Fortunately, his vision was clear enough for him to see Merle standing directly in front of him.

"Whoa, now," Merle said. "Lower that pistol."

"Where is that thing?" Slocum asked.

"It's still nearby, so let's not waste any time before we go after it. That thing slips away and into these woods and we'll lose one hell of an opportunity."

As Merle was talking, he was also helping Slocum to his feet. As soon as he had his legs beneath him, Slocum said, "Did you see where it went after it got me?"

"Thataway," Merle replied while nodding ahead and to the right.

Sure enough, Slocum could hear rustling coming from that direction. Without saying a word, he motioned for Merle to circle around in one direction while he circled in the other. The younger man nodded and both of them set out to close in on the thing that had ambushed them.

The rustling wasn't the same as it had been before. Instead of the persistent rhythm, it was more uneven. More than that, whatever was making the sound wasn't as heavy as what he'd heard before. Wary of walking into another bushwhacking, Slocum kept his body low and his feet on steady ground. He stopped to listen for other noises that weren't caused by the wind or movement of the nearby stream.

The rustling was becoming fainter, which meant Slocum had a choice to make. He could either continue plodding along carefully or he could rush ahead just in case whatever was making those sounds was getting away. Merle had proven to be of some use already, so Slocum put a bit of faith in him and quickened his pace. If he was attacked again or even if he fell, there was someone nearby to back him up. Even so, he couldn't help feeling nervous about blindly stomping forward.

Before long, he became certain that the lighter rustling he was hearing was coming from a spot not too far away and wasn't running away from him.

Soon he saw movement in the bushes. It wasn't much, but some of the lower branches were shaking in time to the sounds he heard. After another couple of steps, he could see the shadow of something moving awkwardly behind those bushes. Rather than trying to see through the tangle of leaves, he hurried around the bushes while looking along the top of his gun barrel.

The foul scent that had assaulted his nose earlier still hung in the air, but only faintly.

Merle exploded through another batch of bushes with his own gun drawn. When he saw Slocum, he immediately looked down at the ground between both of them. A fawn lay there, slashed open across the belly and chest, kicking its legs against the bushes as the last bit of life drained out of it.

"What the hell?" Merle grunted.

"You find anything else?" Slocum asked.

"No. I just heard this, same as you."

Holstering his gun, Slocum crouched down to get a better look at the fawn. "Why don't you see if you can find that thing? I want to have a look at this."

Merle obviously had something to say, but held on to it so he could rush into the woods to pick up the trail of what had brought them out there in the first place.

Although Slocum would have liked for Merle to get close enough to put that animal down or at least wound it, he didn't get his hopes up.

14

After all the commotion, all the yelling and running, Slocum arrived back at the small clearing dragging the dead fawn behind him. Darryl sat on the half-buried log, sipping from his mason jar without a care in the world.

"Enjoying the day?" Slocum asked.

Darryl craned his neck to look up and around at the sky that was showing through the leafy canopy above him. "Now that you mention it, today sure is a nice one."

Slocum dragged the fawn the rest of the way into the clearing and sat down.

"You need any help with that?" Darryl asked. Making a show of looking over to where the carcass lay, he added, "Oh, I guess you handled it just fine on your own."

"You're a real piece of work," Slocum grunted.

"A real piece of somethin'," Merle added as he entered the clearing through the bushes.

Darryl looked over and raised his mason jar in a salute. "You went chargin' out there and came back empty-handed? I'm ashamed of you, little brother!"

"At least I did something other than sit on my ass drinking that slop water," Merle replied.

"For once, I agree with him," Slocum said while nodding toward Merle. "You find anything out there?"

Merle dropped himself down onto the ground to sit with his legs folded over each other. He then leaned forward and reached into the trunk that had been uncovered when they'd first reached the clearing. "Nah, but I aim to walk back out there and pick up the trail from where it started. Where did you see that thing the first time?"

"I was watering the horses when . . . shit!" Slocum said. "The horses. Someone's got to go back and collect them. Come to think of it, they probably didn't wander off too far from where they were drinking."

"Good," Darryl said after a loud belch. "Then you won't have any trouble finding 'em."

"You're the one that sat back and let us do all the work," Slocum said. "I say you're the one to gather the horses."

"And for once," Merle chimed in, "I agree with him."

Darryl shook his head and screwed the lid back onto the mason jar. "Couple of twitchy sons of bitches, leavin' good horses unattended and expectin' me to clean up the mess."

Watching as Darryl carefully placed the jar back into the trunk, Slocum asked, "What is that stuff anyway?"

"This?" Darryl asked while holding up the jar.

"Yeah. Looks like rusted river water and smells almost as bad."

"This," he said while opening the jar once again, "is a family recipe for taking the edge off a hard night spent drinkin'." He took another swig, wiped his hand across his dripping mouth, and let out a loud, satisfied breath.

"What's in it?"

"You sure you wanna know?"

"Actually . . . no. I'm not. Whatever the recipe is, just keep it in the family. And keep it away from me."

"You'd be changin' your tune if you ever needed it."

"What other remedies do you have in that trunk?" Slocum asked. "Any medicine or such?"

"Nah. Just this. I come out here hurtin' from being drunk

more often than I'm hurtin' from anything else. Judging by the looks of you two, though, we should probably start keeping a whole mess of bandages in here."

"Don't worry about us," Merle snapped.

The front of Merle's shirt was torn in two places. Only one of the rips showed a bloody scratch while the others barely exposed Merle's undershirt. "You all right?" Slocum asked.

"This ain't nothin' but a nick," Merle replied while slapping his chest. "I cut myself shaving worse than that. How about you?"

Until now, Slocum had been content to leave his chest be. It was aching somewhat when he drew too deep of a breath, but nothing seemed to be broken. He pressed a hand against the spot where he'd been hit when knocked down to verify that his first guess was mostly accurate. "I'll be fine."

"You probably should come along with us to get the horses. I don't know exactly where that thing was when you saw it."

"I didn't see much, really. I took the horses straight to the stream, crossed it to the wide spot on the shore, and saw something moving across and about a yard or two to the right."

"That the best you can tell me?"

After thinking it over, Slocum said, "Yeah. That's about it."

Merle nodded to himself. "I suppose that's enough. These bushes are pretty thick out here, though. I'm not expectin' to find much in the way of tracks."

"Just do what you can. I want to have a look at this carcass."

"You think there's something to see?" Merle asked.

"I'll find out shortly."

"I'll send Darryl back straightaway with the horses. After that, unless I find some tracks, I say we keep going to Fall Pass. I know another trail we can take that cuts through a part of these woods that's closer to the direction where that thing took off runnin'. That thing will most likely head back to its regular hunting grounds."

"Sounds like a plan."

Merle headed back into the woods as his brother shouted for him in the distance. "Keep yer damn shirt on," he replied. "I'm comin'."

Now that the log was vacated, Slocum took a seat on it and rested his elbows upon his knees. He only needed a few moments to catch his breath, but hadn't wanted to take them while he was under the brothers' scrutiny. He tested the waters by pulling in as large a breath as he could while straightening his back. His chest ached as it had before, but still no shooting pains or anything else that might make him think his injuries were anything but superficial.

Then he shifted his attention to the fawn that had been killed not too far from the clearing. At first glance, the main thing to catch his eye was the slashes across its body that had caused it to bleed out. Slocum pulled a hunting knife from its scabbard on his belt so he could move the flaps of skin and get a better look at the edges that had been cut. They were sliced clean and deep. So deep, in fact, that the fawn's body bent at an awkward angle due to several major sections of bone that had been sliced clean through. The wounds looked more severe than the ones on Edgar or Dave, but that was only because there was so much less meat on a fawn than a man. Studying the wounds carefully, Slocum figured whatever had inflicted them would have ripped up a man about as badly as those two that had been found and brought back to the mill.

Next, Slocum took a closer look at something that had caught his attention while dragging the fawn back to the clearing. There was something peculiar about the way its legs dangled from its torso. They wobbled and bent at spots other than the joints, and when he felt them each one by one, Slocum could tell three out of four of them were broken. More than that, the bones had been snapped all the way through below the knee.

Slocum pushed back some of the fur on the fawn's legs to get a closer look. He wasn't at all surprised to find spots at the point of each break where blood had been drawn and flesh had been stripped away. The only reason he hadn't seen it before was because of all the dirt that had stuck to the blood to make the wound partially blend in with the color of the fawn's coat.

"Whatever it is, it's gone," Merle said as he reentered the clearing.

His brother was behind him and he led all three horses into the clearing by the reins. "Ain't no sign of it. I can verify that much."

"Yeah," Slocum said skeptically. "You two were sure gone long enough to be real thorough about your search."

"I can tell you're bein' a wiseass," Darryl said.

Slocum stood up and said, "Wasn't really trying to hide it. Why don't you take a look at that?"

When Slocum nudged the fawn with his toe, Merle was the one to step forward and examine it. After less than two seconds, he looked up and said, "Looks like a dead deer. Small one."

"Ha!" Darryl bellowed. "Sounds like another wiseass!"

"Take a closer look," Slocum said. "Specifically, the legs."

Merle was shaking his head, but stooped down to get a closer look as requested. He lifted one hoof off the ground, shook it, and then squinted at it a bit closer. "It's busted in two." Peeling back the fur as Slocum had done, he added, "Looks like it was caught in something."

"That's what I was thinking."

"Let me have a look-see," Darryl grunted. He walked over to the fawn to look down and over his brother's shoulder. Straightening up again, he said, "Bear trap."

"Yeah," Merle said. "Or something along those lines. Bear trap might have taken its leg clean off, but it's close."

"I didn't see any traps. Did you?" Slocum asked.

"No, but that don't mean they ain't there. No trap worth a damn can be seen plain as day."

"True. Now take a look at the wounds along its body."

Once again, Darryl leaned over without stooping to get much closer to the fawn. "Looks torn to hell to me," he sneered.

"Shut up if you're gonna be so damn ignorant," Merle said. "I see what he's gettin' at."

"Then why don't you tell me?"

Merle looked over at Slocum. "These slices are too clean to have been done by an animal."

"Exactly," Slocum said. "Did you get a look at what was done to those two that were found at Fall Pass and brought back to the mill?"

"No."

"Well, it was pretty close to what you see right here. Only difference was that there were more cuts on a larger body. The edges were the same. Very clean. The wounds were real deep as well."

"Was it laid out the same as these?" Merle asked while holding three fingers out as if he was drawing the slashes across the fawn's body.

"Yep," Slocum replied. "Three cuts on each swipe."

"I got one question," Darryl said. "Which one of you two is gonna cook up that venison for tonight's supper?"

Merle stood up, turned around, and glared at his brother. "If you'd use what's in your head for one damn minute, you'd see what this all means."

"I know what it means," Darryl snapped. "That fawn stumbled into a trap before that beast found it. And when the beast did find it, he finished it off with three claws on each paw."

"It weren't no claws that did this," Darryl said. "Them cuts were done by blades. Take a look for yourself if you don't believe me."

Darryl grunted as he squatted down to take a closer look. After poking and prodding the carcass, he muttered, "I'll be damned. It does look like the work of a knife. Whoever was swingin' it sure put some muscle behind it, too. Of course," he added while standing up and wiping his hands upon his trousers, "it don't rule out the Beast of Fall Pass. That thing ain't exactly some common animal."

"What we found out in them woods wasn't no animal," Merle said with certainty. "It acted more like something that was huntin' us instead of the other way around."

"And it sounded like it was wounded," Slocum added. "It wheezed when it was running. A wounded animal gets angry and fierce when it's hurt or sick. Something that ripped apart those men wouldn't have just run away when it found two more of us. That doesn't make sense for any animal."

"Not to mention that there ain't no predator alive that would abandon a perfectly good kill like this right here," Darryl said while looking down at the fawn.

"So I suppose that means we're not dealing with an animal," Slocum said.

"Man or beast," Darryl snarled, "we're still hunting it down and dragging it back to town. Everything we know about the damn thing tells us it makes its home near Fall Pass. Let's get out there and commence the hunt."

15

The ride to Fall Pass wasn't a long one. The three of them made it there in just over an hour, even with the detour they'd taken. According to what Rob Ploughman had told Slocum shortly after he'd brought the wounded men back to the mill, he'd found them along Fall Pass less than a quarter mile from the spot where it met up with the trail that led into Bennsonn. It didn't take a tracker to find that spot since there were still plenty of broken tree branches, trampled bushes, and shreds of clothing scattered on the ground.

After dismounting, Darryl approached a spot along the side of the trail where the dirt had been disturbed and stained by enough blood to leave its mark on the earth. He squatted down, touched the ground with his fingertips, and then turned his gaze to the nearby bushes. "Looks like a damn parade came through that tangle of brush," he said. "Them wounded men probably crawled through there and something else crawled out along with 'em before turning around and heading straight back into the woods."

"You two are the hunters," Slocum said. "I know when to step aside and let a man do his work."

The brothers looked at each other as if they were expecting

118

some sort of resistance from Slocum on that subject. Then, with a shrug, they both tethered their horses to a tree and started rummaging through their saddlebags. From what Slocum could tell, the items they'd taken from the trunk in the clearing weren't anything special. Darryl and Merle each equipped themselves with hunting knives and firearms ranging from shotguns to rifles. Slocum could tell by the way they handled those things that they weren't just weapons, however. They were *their* weapons.

Any man tended to work better with tools that felt more familiar in his hands. When it came to a gun or knife, things that a man used to defend his very life, even the smallest elements could make a difference. Slocum knew all too well that a shot could be fired a hair quicker if he was more familiar with the weight, balance, and performance of the gun in his hand. A knife was similar in many respects. There were also elements that some might count as superstitions when it came to weapons that had been with him for many years. Whether a pistol or knife could be considered a lucky charm, believing as such could give a man an edge in a fight by making him less hesitant to make a move.

Once the brothers had armed themselves, they headed into the woods. Darryl was much steadier on his feet, not seeming to feel even the slightest impairment from the previous night's drinking. If the swill in that mason jar truly set him straight in that respect, the detour had been more than worth the effort.

"You gonna follow along or do you want to stay with the horses while me and Darryl take a look around?" Merle asked.

"I'll let you two work," Slocum said. "But I'm not just going to hang back and watch the horses. I'll ride further along the trail and see what I can see. Let's meet back here in a few hours."

"Take all the time you need," Darryl said with a dismissing wave. "Or don't come back at all."

"A few hours," Merle said. "We'll put together what we each found and find a way to hunt this killer."

Slocum nodded and flicked his reins to get his horse moving. Darryl and Merle both ventured into the surrounding woods, disappearing almost immediately as if they'd been born and raised somewhere among those trees.

Slocum wasn't so concerned with covering ground as he was with simply getting a feel for his surroundings. He'd heard of Fall Pass before mention of the beast, but hadn't actually traveled it since he'd been in Bennsonn. There were trees encroaching on all sides and ruts in the ground from what must have been fairly consistent trips back and forth with heavily laden wagons. It was no wonder there were so many frightening stories about that stretch of road. Slocum could only imagine how dark it got once there was no sunlight trying to pierce the upper layers of leaves or the sounds that could be heard from all the insects and animals living beneath the green roof.

After riding less than a hundred yards down the trail, Slocum pulled back on his reins to bring his horse to a stop. He then dismounted and walked to the edge of the trail, where he could stand with his back to the section of trees where Darryl and Merle were most likely hunting. Once there, he did exactly what he'd specifically told the two brothers that he would not do. Slocum stayed put and watched his horse.

Slocum had gotten a hunch as to the best strategy for crossing paths with the killer again. If the beast was an animal, then the Beasley brothers truly were best suited to find it and Slocum should just stand back to let the hunters go about their job.

If the thing that had attacked those two men was a man, then there were other things to consider. After crossing paths with the beast at that stream, Slocum already knew he and the other two were being watched. It was simply too big of a coincidence for him to have crossed paths so soon with the very thing they'd been hunting. Most likely, the road from the mill itself was being watched and the three horses had been spotted soon after putting Bennsonn behind them.

The idea for Slocum to wander off on his own and wait idly came when he'd watched the two brothers prepare all those guns and knives for their venture into the woods. He had no doubt they knew how to hunt, but going after a man was much different than going after an animal. Things took another turn completely if the man knew he was being hunted.

After less than an hour of waiting, Slocum felt the hairs stand up on the back of his neck. The peculiar feeling that he was being watched had saved his skin too many times for him to start ignoring it now. He listened intently for anything that was out of place. What he heard wasn't much, but it was enough to cause him to pivot around on the balls of his feet while drawing the Remington from its holster at his side.

At first, he thought his instincts had led him astray. Such a thing was uncommon, but not unheard of. Slocum's eyes quickly found some branches that had been disturbed and a shadow that didn't seem to belong between a few waist-high bushes.

"Come on out of there," he said while pointing his gun at the vague shape. "I know you've been following us, so show yourself or I start shooting."

The shape was only slightly shorter than the bushes in which it sought refuge. Since its edges blended in with the surrounding foliage so well, it was difficult for Slocum to pick out where the shape ended and where the bushes began. What caught his attention even more was the smell drifting through the air. It was fainter than it had been when he and Merle had been jumped near that stream, but putrid enough to be recognizable.

"All right, then," Slocum warned as he thumbed back the Remington's hammer. "I'll just put you down and have a look at the carcass when I drag it out into the open."

The voice that emerged from that shadow wasn't at all what Slocum had been expecting. It was meek and grating as it said, "It weren't s'posed to happen."

"What wasn't supposed to happen?"

"Them fellers," the shadow said. As a breath was drawn, it made a very familiar wheezing sound. "They weren't s'posed to die."

"You mean those two men that were left on the side of the road."

"Them and the other one."

Slocum thought for a moment and quickly came up with the

name he'd been after. "Abner Woodley," he said. "The man who drove the cart carrying the other two back into town mentioned someone else had been with those two when he found them. His name was Abner Woodley."

"I don't know no names."

"So you're telling me he's dead?"

The shadow moved forward an inch or two, which was just enough for Slocum to get a partial look at a dirty face covered by a tangled mess of leaves. Dirt was encrusted into a beard that was matted down in some places and practically exploding from his chin in others. "That ain't what I said. I said it weren't supposed to die . . . that they . . . weren't s'posed to die."

"One of them is probably dead by now," Slocum said as he tried to make out more of what was in front of him. "Another should pull through. Where's the third man? The one who was with the other two."

"He gone."

"Why don't you show yourself?"

The thing that took a few hesitant steps from the bushes was a man, but just barely. He hunched forward and took slow, shuffling movements as if every muscle in his body was required to move him a few inches. The more Slocum saw of him, the less certain he was of what he was looking at. The man's face was wide, round, and covered in so much dirt that it was hard to distinguish it from the whiskers of his thick, bushy beard. His shoulders were wide as well and covered in thick layers of fur. Furs were also wrapped around his feet by lengths of rope to form crude boots. Pointing at Slocum with his left hand, he kept his right tucked away beneath the fur pelts stitched together to form something of a cloak.

"You tell them others I ain't done nothin' wrong," the man-thing said.

"Were you the one who attacked those men?" Slocum asked. When an answer wasn't forthcoming, he added, "You sure smell like the one I was chasing earlier."

"I came for supper."

"You mean the deer?"

The man nodded. "Three deer. Two big. One little. I wanted to collect 'em and skin 'em."

"That's all you were up to? You sure you weren't watching the road leading from town out to Fall Pass?"

The man's face scrunched into an expression showing vague hints of recognition. "I gotta watch that road. Horses been comin' out more and more. I had to warn 'em."

"Warn who?"

"Thems in that town!" the man said with mounting urgency. "This here is the beast's woods! Ain't no room for more!"

"Did you try to tell the others?" Slocum asked as he inched closer to the strange man.

"I told 'em. I told 'em. I *told 'em!*" As he shouted that last set of words, the man brought his right arm out from where he'd been hiding it. Like every other part of him, that arm was filthy and covered in patches of fur. His fist was caked in mud, and the first thing to catch Slocum's attention when that fist was shaken at him was the set of three long gleaming claws protruding from the man's hand. "Them others had to tell the rest!"

"Tell them what?" Slocum asked in a voice he tried to keep calm.

"I told 'em what needed to be said! I wrote it on their faces," the man said while swiping the air with the three claws. "I carved it into them's backs and fronts and arms and legs!" With every word that came out of his mouth, the filthy man became louder, shakier, and somehow larger. He'd shuffled from the bushes like a cripple, but when he straightened up and extended his arms and legs, he seemed to almost double in size.

"Tell me your name," Slocum said. His intention was to try and defuse the man before he worked himself into a lather. Under the circumstances, and with the other man literally shaking in anticipation of spilling blood, the feeble request was the best Slocum could manage.

Suddenly, the man stopped his ranting. His eyes were wide as saucers set within his face and his mouth hung open like a crooked chasm partly filled with rotten teeth. He wheeled around, slicing the air with his claws while putting his back to

Slocum. Before Slocum could take advantage of the situation, the man lunged toward the bushes and was gone as quickly as if the woods themselves had swallowed him whole.

Slocum reminded himself about how quickly the wild man had moved through the woods earlier that day and how easily he'd gotten the drop on him. "God damn it," he growled while charging through the bushes in the wild man's wake.

Certainly there was a chance that the man could get the drop on him again, but Slocum knew all too well that the man could also get away from him just as quickly. Being in the filthy predator's familiar territory wasn't a consideration because the entirety of the woods was surely his stomping ground. The only way to maintain any semblance of control in the hunt was to remain on the offensive. The alternative was to let the wild man go to take another swipe at him later. Better to charge into the fight head-on than be bushwhacked when his back was turned.

Slocum's worries about being attacked the moment he came through the bushes were laid to rest when he cleared the foliage to find no trace of the other man. Since a few simple words had somehow lit the wild man's fuse and he didn't have any other cards to play, Slocum shouted into the woods, "Who are you? I asked your name!"

Surprisingly enough, he got an answer.

"I ain't no name!"

The response didn't make much sense, but it gave Slocum a direction in which to run. Gripping his Remington and holding it at the ready, he hurried through the woods as quickly as he dared. It was a tricky thing to navigate the rugged, unfamiliar terrain. As he continued to run, Slocum eventually heard the sounds he'd been hoping for.

The snapping of branches and pounding of feet were far away at first, but closed in awfully quick.

"That you, Slocum?" Merle shouted from deeper within the woods.

"I found our killer!" Slocum shouted. "Circle around and cut him off!"

"I ain't no killer!" the wild man hollered. "I'm a damn killer, is what I is!" It seemed the more he tried to speak, the less sense he made. Even so, that didn't hamper his ability to rush through the woods. As the trees and brush grew thicker, he found ways to pull even farther away from Slocum.

The first time Slocum found a clearer path through the trees, he pumped his legs even harder to try and build up some more speed as he cut around to come at the fleeing wild man from a different angle. Instead of gaining any ground, he lost some while losing sight of the wild man.

"I think I see ya!" Merle shouted.

"He's getting away!" Slocum replied.

There was more rustling in the bushes farther ahead, followed by the impact of something heavy slamming against the ground amid a pained wheeze.

"Over here, the both of you," Darryl shouted.

Slocum had to adjust his path accordingly, but soon caught sight of two bulky figures wrestling in the dirt. If he hadn't already seen the wild man, Slocum might have thought Darryl was fighting with a small bear. From other angles, it even seemed he was rolling around with a mess of old pelts.

Despite the chaos of the scuffle, Darryl gained the upper hand fairly quickly. He grabbed hold of the other man's crude cloak and slammed him onto his back. The instant he moved one hand to his belt to draw a hunting knife from one of the scabbards hanging at his side, Darryl was forced to defend himself from a powerful slash.

The wild man let out a trembling howl as he swung his right fist at Darryl's face. Spotting the claws extending from the other man's fist, Darryl cursed loudly and pitched himself backward in order to avoid getting his face ripped off the front of his skull. His movement may not have looked pretty, but it did the job. Not only did he clear a path for the clawed hand, but he propped himself up onto one knee with his right hand wrapped tightly around the grip of a hunting knife.

"You wanna dance, ya mangy dog?" Darryl sneered as he took a few quick jabs with the knife. "Let's dance."

The wild man had pure savagery on his side, and all of his

swings were powered by every muscle at his disposal. The attacks were unfocused, however, and Darryl avoided them with minimal effort. Each time those claws came his way, Darryl leaned or ducked without taking his eyes off the man in front of him.

Rushing at the wild man would have been akin to throwing himself face first onto one of the saws back at the mill, so Slocum held his ground. He took aim with the Remington and cursed under his breath as his target bobbed, swayed, and was periodically blocked by Darryl.

Strangely enough, tangling with a feral beast caused Darryl to be calmer than he'd been in the short time Slocum had known him. Instead of playing the wild man's game, he stayed just out of harm's way while taking the occasional poke with his knife. After tapping the tip of the blade against a thick mass of furs on his opponent's side, Darryl waited for the wild man to respond. When the wild man swung in the direction of that most recent jab from the hunting knife, Darryl leaned the opposite way and took a vicious swing at him.

If Darryl had been facing most anyone else, the slash would have opened one hell of a nasty cut. Although the blade cut through some layers of fur surrounding the wild man's torso, it was impossible to tell if any damage was done. The wild man wailed and attacked again, spurred on by pure ferocity. Any pain from Darryl's attack only added fuel to his fire.

"Down!" Merle shouted from somewhere out of Slocum's line of sight.

Whether or not Darryl could see his brother, he followed his directions by dropping straight down.

The wild man twisted around to find his prey, raised his clawed hand, and threw himself at Darryl while flailing with both arms.

Slocum recognized the report from the shot that was fired as having come from Merle's hunting rifle. A bullet hissed through the air, clipping the edge of one of the wild man's shoulders. It would have been a good shot on any other target, but trying to hit this one square was like trying to hit a moth dead center as it was blown on a stiff breeze. Even though Merle hadn't hit anything vital, the impact of his round caused the wild man to twist away from Darryl and land awkwardly on his side.

The wild man popped up while swinging his claws to meet Darryl's hunting knife amid a shower of sparks, causing both of them to recoil. While the wild man was reeling and before he could throw his entire body into another attack, he was hit by another bullet. This one caught him in the middle of his right arm, drilling through that elbow and bringing a pained cry from the back of his throat.

Slocum's Remington was smoking from the shot he'd just fired and he hurried forward while shouting, "I got him, Darryl. Stand aside."

Darryl's eyes were set on the man in front of him and he lunged at the wild man with a powerful swing of his hunting knife. Once again, the blade raked across layers of fur padding.

"I said stand aside!" Slocum demanded.

"The hell I will," Darryl said. "This crazy bastard tried to kill me!"

"He won't swing that arm again. Stand aside."

Merle stepped forward with his hunting rifle at his shoulder. "He makes one move and I'll put him down," he swore.

"It's over," Slocum declared. "We're not executing this man."

Looking around and taking some satisfaction from how the fight had concluded, Darryl got the last word by driving his left fist straight into the wild man's face to knock him out. "*Now* it's over," he sneered.

16

All three of the hunters were in good spirits after overpowering the wild man. Merle held him at gunpoint while Slocum and Darryl hurried to get the man's wrists and ankles bound with several lengths of rope. Even though the prisoner didn't show the first hint of waking up through the entire process, all of the men worked as if he were still thrashing and swinging his claws at them. When they were finished, the three of them gazed down at their prisoner as though they still weren't sure whether he was man or beast.

"What now?" Merle asked.

"What do you mean, what now?" Darryl grunted. "We take him back to town and collect our pay."

"You think there's any more of them?"

Slocum had been wondering about that himself. So far, he had yet to arrive at a conclusion. "There could be, I suppose," he said. "But I would imagine any more would have come along to help this one by now."

Giving the prisoner a spiteful kick, Darryl said, "This one's out of his damn mind. Anyone else that throws in with him would have to be just as crazy. There ain't no allegiances with crazy folks."

"So . . . what does that mean?" Merle asked.

"It means the same as the last question you asked, little brother. We drag this one in and collect our pay. We were supposed to hunt down whatever sliced up them two mill workers. Judging by the looks of this one here, I'd say we found him. They want someone to turn over every rock and check in every stump of these damn woods, they'll have to pay a whole lot more."

"How do we know this one hurt them other men?" Darryl asked.

"Let's just get him loaded onto a horse," Slocum said. "It'll be a whole lot easier to do that now than when he's awake." Knowing that the brothers needed some extra prodding before they would accept any order, he added, "Also, if there are any more of them like him out here, we probably don't want to be standing around in these woods any longer than we need to."

"Fine," Darryl said, "but you're helpin' me load him."

"Let's get to it."

Slocum grabbed the unconscious prisoner beneath his arms while Darryl lifted his legs. Between the two of them, they carried him back to where the horses were waiting and draped him over the back of Merle's tan and brown mare. The prisoner had stirred a bit during the process, but was still out like a wet lantern wick as they started heading down Fall Pass on their way to the trail that would take them back to Bennsonn.

Darryl rode at the front of the small group so he could keep an eye on the trail ahead while the other two followed him. Instead of riding single file, Slocum rode alongside Merle so he could keep close watch on the younger brother's unconscious passenger.

Although all three of them wanted to put those woods behind them as quickly as possible, they rode at a steady pace. The horses walked along as the men on their backs glanced in every direction, searching for the source of every sound that came along. Even after they were no longer riding on Fall Pass, Merle continued to look over his shoulder.

When Slocum noticed the younger man glancing down at who was strapped across his horse's back, he asked, "What's wrong? Is he starting to come around?"

"Why?" Merle asked quickly. "Did you see something?"

"No. The way you keep looking back at him, I thought maybe you felt him kick."

"Oh. No, I didn't feel nothing."

"So," Merle asked quietly, "you think this is really the ass-hole that cut up them men?"

"I'd say so. Those blades he's holding could have made wounds in the same pattern as the ones on those men and they sure as hell look sharp enough to get the job done."

Leaning in a bit and dropping his voice so it couldn't be so easily heard by his older brother, Merle asked, "You're certain them are blades? They sure look like claws to me."

Slocum had had plenty of time to look at the curved weapons while tying up the wild man and carrying him to the horse. Then, like now, all he could see were curved, sharpened claws protruding from between the fingers of the prisoner's right hand, but his fist was clenched so tightly that Slocum couldn't see much more than that.

They weren't like an animal's claws since they were obviously forged from some kind of metal. The edges had been sharpened and had the scoring marks to prove it. Leaning over, Slocum held on to his saddle horn with one hand and reached for the prisoner with his other. "One way to find out for certain what they are," he said while grabbing the wild man's hand.

Merle winced and looked up at his brother as though he was expecting to get reprimanded. Instead, Darryl was preoccupied by watching the trail ahead while drinking from his mason jar.

It was difficult for Slocum to find a spot to grab the metal weapons in the wild man's hand without getting cut in the process. The prisoner's fist was still clenched tightly shut. Finally, Slocum was able to get a grip on the weapon by putting his own fingers between the claws in much the same way that the prisoner was gripping them. From there, he pulled and twisted the claws until the fingers wrapped around them finally started to loosen. Pulling one last time with his hand as well as his entire upper body while leaning back, Slocum managed to pry the claws free.

Holding them up so Merle could see, Slocum said, "Well, I guess that answers one question."

The claws were indeed blades instead of anything growing from the man's fist. Long knives, sharpened along one edge, were connected at the bottom to a wooden handle wrapped in leather straps. Not only was the grip contoured to match the hand that held them, but the leather was darkened and bloody after having been gripped for such a long time. In fact, considering how the prisoner's fingers were still curled into the shape they'd been when clutching the weapon, Slocum guessed the wild man rarely let his weapon go.

"Nasty piece of work," Slocum said. "See for yourself."

When Slocum tossed the weapon over to him, Merle was just quick enough to catch it. Even though he'd almost cut himself on the blades, he seemed more than a little relieved when he got a good look at the weapon to verify it had indeed been crafted from nothing more than wood and iron. "This is one crazy son of a bitch. Hey, Darryl! Look here at these knives!"

Darryl turned around to look over his shoulder. "You finally pry them from his hand? Thought you'd never work up the courage."

"You were just as nervous as I was."

"Sure, when them blades were comin' at my face! Truth is, little brother, you've always been the nervous and superstitious one in the family. I imagine you thought this whole time he had them blades popping out from his arm!" Darryl let out a long laugh that shook his entire body while his brother clenched his jaw shut tight and stared daggers at his back.

They rode awhile longer before Darryl led them down the same branch in the trail they'd taken before.

"Where do you think you're going?" Slocum asked.

"Waterin' the horses," Darryl replied.

"We can make it back to town without watering the horses. We're losing daylight."

"What's the matter, Slocum? Don't you like your horse?"

"I like him just fine. What I don't like is tacking more time onto this ride than what's necessary. You can't have drunk so much whiskey that you still need whatever witch's brew is in that mason jar."

"Everything we took from there needs to be put back," Darryl said. "Otherwise, me and Merle will just have to drag ourselves out here again to do it some other time."

As much as Slocum wanted to argue, he knew that would only cause more grief and waste more time. Since the prisoner was strapped to Merle's horse and not his own, Slocum grudgingly went along with them as they headed for the clearing near the stream.

Darryl was out of his saddle and leading his horse through the now-familiar bushes like a kid running into a candy store. By the time Slocum and Merle had caught up to him, Darryl had already uncovered the trunk and was fishing out a bottle of clear liquor that had most likely been brewed in a bathtub.

Slocum volunteered to take the horses to the stream, and Darryl wasn't inclined to argue. After placating his brother by sharing a drink with him, Merle hurried to catch up to him. Slocum wasn't wound as tightly as he had been before, but he still almost drew his pistol when Merle rushed from the bushes to come straight at him.

"He wake up yet?" Merle asked.

Slocum moved his hand away from his holster and continued what he'd been doing before Merle had arrived. "Doesn't look like it," Slocum said while searching the wild man's clothing for pockets. "But I'm starting to think he's just asleep. Darryl didn't hit him that hard."

"He was pretty worked up. One of our aunts was touched in the head, and she tended to keel over every now and again to sleep for the better part of a day. She was dead to the world when that happened."

Since Merle was trying to be earnest, Slocum kept his comments to himself regarding his lack of surprise that someone so close to the brothers on their family tree was touched in the head. "Could just be he's playing possum," Slocum said.

Wincing, Merle said, "From the stench comin' off of this one, *dead* possum is more like it."

Slowly, a grin found its way onto Slocum's face. "Since we're already stopped here, why don't we make the rest of our ride a little easier?"

Merle didn't know exactly what Slocum was getting at until he noticed the way Slocum was eyeing the stream. "I'll take his legs?"

"And I'll take his arms."

"If I have to smell that stench for one more minute, I'm gonna puke up everything I ate for the last week."

"I second that motion," Slocum said before grabbing the prisoner once more beneath the arms. Both he and Merle were laughing as they picked up the wild man and took him off the back of Merle's horse.

As it turned out, the wild man was indeed playing possum. Either that, or he just happened to snap his eyes open while saying, "You toss me into that water and I'll kill you!"

"Yeah, yeah," Slocum grunted as he carried him toward the stream. "At least we'll die without having to smell you and that god-awful fur you got wrapped around yourself."

By now, the wild man was suspended over the water and swaying back and forth thanks to the men holding him from both ends. He wriggled like a worm on a hook, screaming as if the stream were a cauldron of boiling oil. At the height of his third swing, he was released and dropped in. The water was just deep enough to cover him and shallow enough to give him a jarring welcome when he landed on the mossy submerged rocks.

"What in the hell are you two doin'?" Darryl asked as he charged from the bushes with his gun drawn.

Still grinning from ear to ear, Slocum replied, "Giving our friend a much-needed bath."

"You're all gonna die!" the wild man shouted as he sat straight up and shook his head like a shaggy dog.

Darryl looked down at him and grimaced at the growing cloud of filth spreading from the prisoner on all sides. "Damn! You're gonna poison the horses."

"Hadn't thought of that," Slocum admitted. "Maybe we should drag him out of there."

"Nah, leave him in," Darryl said. "Maybe he won't be so surly once we get him out of them stinkin' skins he's wearing."

"You can't take these off!" the prisoner said. "They're part of me! They keep me alive!"

Merle waded into the water so he could stand directly in front of the prisoner. "You know somethin'? I'd feel a bit of compassion for you if you hadn't used them blades to cut apart at least two men before trying to gut me and my brother like a damn fish." With that, he grabbed a handful of the prisoner's hair and dunked him under the water.

Suddenly, Slocum realized he'd almost forgotten a very important piece of their job out in those woods. When Merle pulled the prisoner back up again, Slocum asked, "You want out of that water?"

"Yeah!" the prisoner replied.

"You want to keep them smelly skins of yours?"

"I need them!"

"Then tell me where that third man is."

Merle and Darryl looked at each other with vaguely surprised expressions. In the midst of the hunt and everything that had happened along the way, they must have let that detail slip from their minds as well.

"What third man?" the wild man asked.

"There was another man who was with the two that you cut up and left near the trail at Fall Pass. He was a tracker named Abner Woodley."

"I recall that name," the wild man said. "The fella driving the cart spoke it."

"Where is he?"

"He went after the beast."

"What did you do to him?" The only answer he got was a wide-eyed stare, so Slocum stepped up closer to him and said, "You can tell us now and make it easier or you can tell the law after they beat it out of you. Understand?"

Eventually, the wild man wrapped his arms around himself and said, "These skins are mine! I killed for 'em and I'll kill you, bitch bastards sons of whores goddamn—"

Darryl cut him off with a swift right cross that knocked him back into the water. When he pulled him out again, the wild man continued to spit obscenities as if they were the only words in his language. Finally, Slocum shut him up by knocking the butt of his pistol against the prisoner's temple. Once the wild man sagged backward, Merle had to hold him up to keep him from drowning in the shallow stream.

"That's about all I could stomach," Darryl said while rubbing his knuckles. "Let's get these damn skins off'a him so we can make the rest of the ride without gagging." Then Darryl pulled the hunting knife from its scabbard and proceeded to slice the wild man's wrappings off as if he were skinning a buck.

Since Darryl seemed content to do the job on his own, Slocum left him to it. Turning to Merle, he asked, "Did Womack tell you about Abner Woodley?"

"Yeah."

"Did you happen to look for him while you were searching the spot where those bodies were found?"

"That's what I forgot to tell you," Merle replied. "We found some tracks that led into the woods, but they led straight across some rocky ground and through a bunch of dead leaves. I'm guessin' he didn't want to be found."

"Covered his own tracks?"

Merle nodded. "Probably didn't want this one here tracking him down," he said while nodding toward the prisoner. "We can keep lookin', but it won't be easy. There weren't no blood or anything else to show he was dead or badly hurt, so it may be easier to let him come back to town on his own."

"He's probably there already," Darryl said as he lifted the wild man from the stream. All that remained of the prisoner's skins was a few wet shreds that had gotten snagged beneath the ropes around his wrists and ankles. Hoisting the drenched, near-naked man over one shoulder, Darryl added, "I heard a thing or two about Abner. Hell of a tracker. If anyone had a better chance of finding this beast, it's him. Of course, I won't complain about this beast finding us."

If Bennsonn had been any farther away, Slocum would have

opted to stay put and continue looking for the remaining man
who had been left in the woods. But since nobody had found
anything to make him believe Abner was hurt, he decided to
put the wild man away first and come back for Abner
tomorrow.

Now that the stinking skins were gone and the prisoner was
once again quiet, the ride into town was as pleasant as it was
short.

17

When the solitary rider entered town, he didn't attract much notice. He was just another man arriving in Bennsonn on business of his own. Most of the people who looked his way didn't find enough of interest to keep their eyes on him. Those who watched him longer than that were encouraged to turn another way when the man returned their stare with cold, dark eyes.

He sat tall in his saddle, shifting his weight with every one of his horse's steps as if he'd been riding one trail or another for most of his life. He was of average height and build, wrapped in dusty clothes and a long coat that draped across his horse's back to partially conceal the Spencer rifle carried in his saddle's boot. That wasn't the only weapon on his person. A .45-caliber Smith & Wesson was strapped to his hip and a smaller .32 Colt was tucked in a holster under his left arm. The long, dark brown hair hanging to his shoulders looked more like a cropped mane while the patch of neatly trimmed whiskers covering his upper lip and a small portion of his chin gave him something of a distinguished appearance.

Although he would normally keep his head down when entering unfamiliar territory, he couldn't help looking straight ahead and studying every detail of every sight in front of him.

His eyes darted to and fro, taking note of each face he passed. Instincts honed from passing through more towns than he could count brought him to Bennsonn's saloon district in short order. The first place he saw was a tall, narrow building that looked as if it had been one of the first ones built when the town was founded. A sign painted on the front window said BARKER'S SPIRITS AND SONG. After tying his horse to a post and making sure there was some water in the nearby trough, he patted the animal's nose and walked inside.

Although there were plenty of spirits on display behind the short bar on one side of the room, there were no songs. A piano sat next to a dilapidated stage that, in its prime, would have supported no more than three dancing girls. Now it could barely support its own weight and the piano beside it gathered as much dust on its keys as tobacco juice stains on its base. The man stepped up to the bar and waited to be noticed.

A barkeep standing no more than four feet tall approached him, stepped onto a stool behind the bar, and smiled. "What can I get for you, mister?"

"I'll have a whiskey," the man replied.

"Comin' right up."

Both men's voices echoed within the place since they were the only two there. The clink of bottle meeting glass only made the saloon feel emptier than it already was. After placing the glass of whiskey onto the bar in front of his only customer, the barkeep beamed proudly as if he'd been the one to brew the liquor as well as serve it. "Anything else for you?"

"I'm looking for someone by the name of John Slocum. You know who he is?"

"Mind if I ask who wants to know?"

The man lifted the glass of whiskey to his mouth, tipped it back, and set it down, all without taking his eyes off the man in front of him. "I am," he said smoothly.

"I don't want to start any trouble here."

"What makes you think there's going to be trouble?"

"No offense," the barkeep said, "but you don't strike me as someone looking to reunite with an old friend. You're wearing at least two guns and you chewed on your words when you mentioned the name of the man you were after."

The man nodded slowly. "All right, then." He reached under his coat, opening it to reveal more of the .32 under his arm. The barkeep tensed, paled slightly, and exhaled when a small wad of money was taken out instead of the pistol. The man peeled off one of the bills and set it down. "That's for steering me in the right direction. There'll be more coming if your directions pan out."

"If I'm to give up a good man like that, I'll need a bit more to clear my conscience."

A smile flickered across the man's face, doing nothing to alleviate the tension in the air. "You don't seem all too friendly in regards to that name. You own this place?"

"I do."

"Then it's plain to see that you need every bit of money you can scrape together." The man peeled off a few more bills, but didn't place them on top of the first one just yet. "What can you tell me about John Slocum?"

"He was in a scrape or two over at the Second Saloon just down the street. He works at the mill."

"How do you know him?"

"Does it matter?"

"It does," the man sternly replied, "if you're just feeding me a line of horse manure to get your hands on this money."

Sighing, the barkeep said, "He was after one of my regular customers in regards to some feud between them. I haven't seen that very good customer of mine since, and as you mentioned already," the barkeep added while sweeping his little hand to encompass the saloon, "I don't have many of them to spare. Him coming around to roust one and chase away the others hurt me. If he's got some bit of misery coming from some other direction, that's fine by me. My grandma always told me people get what's coming to them one way or another."

"Well, you keep this," the man said as he put down the money in his hand. "I'm good for my word, so if I catch up to Slocum, I'll be back to pay you the rest."

"Sure. And do me another favor."

Already turning away from the bar, the man stopped and faced the little fellow behind it.

"That regular customer of mine is Lester Quint," the barkeep said. "If you run into him somewhere along the way, let him know it's safe to come back here. I'll even give him a better discount than before."

"I'll do that," the man said. He then tipped his hat and went on his way.

After a short walk down Cedar Street, he spotted the Second Saloon as well as a place called the Axe Handle. The man hadn't forgotten which one he was supposed to go to, but decided to start at the other just to see what he might find. After asking two people a minimum of questions, he got plenty more than he'd bargained for.

"John Slocum?" one of the barkeeps at the Axe Handle replied. "Hell yes, I know him! You a friend of his?"

"That's right," the man replied as he plastered on a somewhat convincing smile. "You know where I can find him?"

"Should be around anytime. Hey, Nellie!"

Following the barkeep's line of sight, the man found a woman with reddish blond hair and generous curves wrapped in a flimsy excuse for a dress. She sauntered over and immediately placed a hand flat upon the man's chest. "What can I do for you, honey?" she purred.

"This one's looking for John Slocum," the barkeep said. "You know where he is?"

"He's been across the street on occasion," she replied. "But I think he rode out to look for the Beast of Fall Pass."

"The what?"

Waving her hand as if she were clearing cobwebs from the air, Nellie said, "Just some myth. Probably nothing but a bear. They should be back anytime. I can think of a few ways to keep you busy while you wait, though."

"I'm sure you could." Taking hold of her wrist before it could reach any farther below his belt, the man asked, "What about Lester Quint?"

"I think I can make you feel a lot better than he could," she told him.

"No doubt about that. I just need to have a word with him. After that, I think I'd like to see you again." He reached into his pocket and found a few dollars, which he then slipped down the front of Nellie's dress. His fingers lingered in the warmth of her cleavage as he said, "Think that'll tide you over until I get back to you?"

Her eyes widened and she shifted her body to ease his hand even farther between her breasts. "That should do nicely. Lester rents one of the houses on Third Avenue. Number six."

"He there now?"

"He doesn't go much of anywhere else ever since Slocum handed him a beating. I think his pride is hurt worse than anything else. Let him know I'm thinking of him, but," she added while fishing out the money, "I'll really be thinking of you instead." She took his hand and placed it between her legs so he could feel the warm spot through her skirts. "Hurry back or I'll have to start without you."

"I'll do that."

"What's your name, honey?"

"I'll introduce myself proper when I get back," he said.

Nellie smiled and waved when he left.

From there, the man went straight to the corner and saw that the intersecting street was Second. He made his way to Third Avenue and spotted a short row of small houses on either side of the street that all looked as if they'd been poured from the same mold. Each had a number nailed to the door, but he took his time before approaching the one he was after.

The man walked slowly down the street, wary of what was happening on either side. Apart from a few children playing nearby and one old woman keeping an eye on them, there wasn't much to see. When he finally did step up to the door of the house bearing the number six, nobody in the vicinity seemed to give a damn.

After knocking on the door, the man heard nothing so he knocked again. A few more seconds passed before he saw a shadow move behind one of the curtained windows. When he knocked a third time, it was hard enough to rattle the door in its frame.

"Get the hell off my damn porch!" someone bellowed from inside.

"You're Lester Quint?"

"Yeah, and I got a shotgun, so get the hell off my porch! I won't ask again!"

"I'd just like a word with you, sir."

The curtain shifted to one side so an angry face could peek out.

"I won't take much of your time," the man promised.

Lester gritted his teeth and moved away from the window. Soon, the door was unlocked and jerked open so he could show himself and the shotgun he'd mentioned to the man on his porch. "You got two seconds," Lester snarled. "Best make 'em count."

"I'm looking for John Slocum and I was told you might be able to help me find him."

"I ain't no friend of that son of a bitch, so I sure as hell ain't gonna help you. Now get to walkin' or I'll cut you in half with this scattergun."

Despite the harsh words and the twin barrels pointed at him, the man smiled and said, "My name is Buck Oberman. I have business to settle with Mr. Slocum."

"What kind of business?"

"This kind," Buck said as he peeled open his coat to show the gun at his side. "And I can assure you, I'm no friend of John Slocum either."

Slowly, Lester stepped aside. "Why don't you come on in?"

18

Most of the time, Slocum didn't mind a day spent in the saddle. In fact, he found it preferable to spending time with most people and would gladly remain under a wide-open sky than cooped up in a room with a bunch of strangers. Still, considering the circumstances of his most recent ride, Slocum was plenty glad to back within Bennsonn's town limits.

It took them a bit longer to get back than it had for them to ride out in the first place on account of the load Merle's horse was carrying. Also, Darryl and Slocum were both preoccupied with searching for any other wild men springing from the trees swinging strange three-bladed knives. No such surprises were in store for them, however. Once they got within sight of town, Darryl had begun lobbying to be the one to take their filthy cargo in to the sheriff's office.

"Go right ahead," Slocum sighed.

Obviously expecting more of a fight, Darryl asked, "You don't mind us taking him in? We can bring you your part of any reward."

"Or you can just tell him to keep it and I'll come get it later."

"We won't cheat you, you know."

"I know," Slocum said. "Wasn't even thinking that."

143

Darryl blinked, turned away, turned back, and blinked again. Finally, he grumbled and rode on.

Shaking his head as he followed, Merle said, "I'll make sure your part of the money stays put. Will you be staying in town for a spell?"

"Yeah. If you need anything, leave word at the Morrison House."

"I was thinking we could split a bottle of whiskey."

Slocum nodded. "Sounds good. In fact, I think I'll get a jump on it at the first saloon to strike my fancy."

"Don't spread too many wild stories about subduing the beast until we get back to lend our two cents."

"I'll try."

Merle followed his brother to Sheriff Krueger's office, and Slocum rode to the stable to put his horse up for the night. Then he walked to the Axe Handle, which was nearby. He stopped a few steps shy of the saloon's front door, thinking about the card games he'd been playing there. While he enjoyed a good game of poker, Slocum wasn't in the mood to sit at a table with a bunch of gamblers who were out to fleece him. All he wanted was to have a drink or two. When his eyes drifted toward the Second Saloon across the street, he thought how nice it would be to have that drink with some pleasant company.

The Second Saloon wasn't exactly quiet. Slocum walked inside, looked over at the faro tables, and saw all three of them were being run by dealers that weren't half as pretty as Eliza. On the contrary, not one of them was even a lady. All three dealers looked over at him expectantly, hoping he would come to their table and add more to the percentage of the house take they were allowed to claim as their own. Slocum nodded back at them and turned to the bar. He was startled to find Eliza standing there with a smile on her face waiting for him.

"Were you there the whole time?" Slocum asked.

"Yes," Eliza replied with a smirk. "You didn't even notice." She wore a black dress with blue ribbons stitched into a bodice that hugged her form nicely. The dark colors made her skin seem smoother than cream that had been poured over a peach.

The fact that Slocum had overlooked her spoke to just how tired he was.

"Why aren't you at your table?" he asked.

She rolled her eyes. "A few of my players had lucky streaks and Rolf was convinced I was bad luck for the house, so he told me to serve drinks for a while." Her eyes widened and she leaned against the bar to say, "I heard you and the Beasleys went after the Beast of Fall Pass."

"You heard right," he said.

"Did you catch anything?"

"Yep. It stands somewhere close to eight feet tall, walks on two legs, has claws as long as your hand, and fangs that could take a bite out of this bar like it was made from peanut brittle."

Her mouth gaped open and her eyes grew even wider. "Really?" she gasped.

Slocum bathed in the moment for a few seconds before saying, "No. He's just some crazy man dressed in smelly skins swinging some mighty big knives. He did put up quite a fight, though."

Eliza laughed. "Still sounds exciting. When did you get back?"

"Less than an hour ago. I wanted to have a drink and thought I'd come here for it."

"Did you miss me?" she asked shyly.

"Actually, I did come here for you. The way I see it, you owe me at least a steak dinner."

"How do you figure?"

"You agreed to spend a quiet evening with Lester Quint when you thought he was me," Slocum explained. "Having met Lester, I believe you were cheated from what that evening could have been. And . . . I can tell by the way you're blushing right now that I've touched a nerve."

"I really don't even know you," she said.

"Then let's change that. I can tell you all about the hunt for the beast. Or if you'd like something a little more exciting, I can tell you about the bank robbers I chased out of Cheyenne."

"You . . . chased bank robbers out of Cheyenne?" she asked with no small amount of skepticism.

"Well, not just me. I was riding in a posse, but it's still a hell of a story. Tell you what . . . you come along with me tonight and I'll pay for the steak dinner. I should be able to scrape up some money from the sheriff. Come on, now. Don't make me beg."

The smile that had appeared on her face as a glimmer had grown to something much brighter. Finally, she said, "I suppose that sounds inviting. But I can't just leave my duties here."

"Soldiers have duties," Slocum said. "Mayors have duties. Even parents have duties. Pouring drinks for these folks, as friendly as I'm sure they are, doesn't exactly qualify as a duty. Do you have any young ones waiting for you?"

"Not hardly."

"Then what are we waiting for?" he asked while offering his hand to her across the top of the bar. "You strike me as a woman looking for a good reason to kick her heels up a bit."

Although Eliza hesitated, the glimmer in her eyes told Slocum that she was only trying to think of the quickest way to put that saloon behind her. Before too long, she settled on taking Slocum's hand, hopping up to sit on the bar and swinging her legs over so he could help her come down on the other side.

From out of nowhere, Rolf stomped toward the bar. "What's the meaning of this? Where do you think you're going?"

"She's coming with me," Slocum said. "I'm a paying customer and I demand that she escort me to get something to eat."

"That don't allow her to come and go as she pleases!" Rolf fumed.

"I just returned from risking life and limb for this town," Slocum said without missing a beat. "Two other brave souls and I captured the Beast of Fall Pass, and this generous lady offered to thank me on behalf of this fine establishment!"

Without much of any consideration, Rolf shook his head. "Still don't cut it."

Before Slocum could come up with another grand statement to throw at the barkeep, Eliza said, "I'll make it up to you," and slipped her arm around Slocum's.

Rolf was sputtering, but quickly quieted down when another woman came along to pat him on the back. "Don't get your knickers in a twist," Mary said. "I'll watch the bar. You go along, Eliza. Have a good ol' time."

"She will," Slocum promised.

It had been simple instinct when Slocum had decided to pay a visit to the Second Saloon so he could call on Eliza. Seeing her in that black dress with raven hair framing her pretty face, Slocum felt a different kind of instinct that was even more powerful.

They'd had supper at the steakhouse Slocum visited often enough to be recognized by the owner, who grudgingly agreed to extend him a short line of credit. Slocum and Eliza talked, laughed, and he told her plenty of stories. Just when he thought it was time for him to stop flapping his gums, she gazed at him intently and asked for more.

Upon leaving the steakhouse, Slocum and Eliza took a walk in the cool night air. There was a gentle breeze playing with her hair and the edges of her skirt. Dim light from the stars played beautifully upon her face and arms. Although Slocum didn't rightly know where they were walking, she led him to a small house at the end of a quiet street.

They stepped inside after a few more pleasantries, but didn't venture much farther than the sitting room just beyond her front door. Although she talked about parting ways after a splendid evening, her eyes told a different story. Slocum tested the waters by stepping in a bit closer while placing his hands upon her hips.

"I . . . shouldn't," she whispered while leaning in closer to him.

"Maybe," he said. "Maybe not. But something tells me you want to."

Every breath she took caused her body to swell, which pressed her against him even more. Eliza opened her mouth as if to speak, but no words came out. When Slocum moved in a bit more, she placed her hands on his face and kissed him hungrily. Their tongues quickly started to wander, causing her to moan softly and with mounting passion.

"Not here," she said.

Moving back, even an inch, at that moment was physically painful for Slocum but he somehow managed. "No?"

"No." With a smile, she took his hand and started walking down a short hallway. "In here."

She led him to her bedroom, and when she kissed him again, Eliza gave in to the desire that had been building the entire night. She trembled with anticipation as Slocum pushed her against a wall and started gathering up her skirts so he could reach beneath them. Her hands were busy as well, tugging at his belt buckle and occasionally cupping the growing bulge in his crotch.

"Yes," she sighed once his fingers discovered the moist lips between her legs.

Slocum had pulled aside the layers of her clothing while she'd loosened his jeans enough for them to be pulled down far enough to free his erect member. He pressed her against the wall while taking hold of one of her legs so he could lift it up near his waist. Eliza was feeling his rigid cock, stroking every inch while looking into his eyes. When he moved his hips toward her, she guided him toward her slick opening. Slocum eased into her, causing Eliza to grip his shoulder and draw a sharp breath.

Watching her as he slid in deeper, Slocum was careful not to pump too hard. Once he was all the way inside her, he felt her grind her hips while wrapping both arms around the back of his neck. She smiled hungrily, and Slocum started pumping faster, gliding in and out of her in a building rhythm. Leaning her head back against the wall, Eliza moaned softly.

As good as it felt to be inside her, Slocum wanted more. He reached down to grab her other leg and Eliza hopped up to wrap them both around him. Cupping her ass in both hands, he held her up against the wall and thrust into her harder. Slocum could feel her fingers digging into his neck and shoulders. She leaned her face in close to his and grunted every time he plunged into her. The sound of her building pleasure was music to his ears, and he pumped into her again and again just to see how much she wanted him to give.

Eliza showed no signs of letting up. In fact, the more he drove between her legs, the more she urged him onward with throaty moans and urgent motions with her hips. When he felt that she was gripping him tightly with both arms, Slocum moved away from the wall and carried her to the bed. He remained inside her all the way until lowering her onto the edge of the mattress to set her down. She looked up at him with her legs open and her pussy dripping.

"You're not going to stop, are you?" she asked.

"Not hardly," Slocum replied. Grabbing both of her ankles, he positioned her so her legs rested on his shoulders while he stood facing her. Eliza's backside was on the very edge of the mattress so all he had to do to enter her again was ease forward and slip the tip of his cock between her glistening lips.

Eliza moaned as he filled her with every inch of his hard flesh. She cried out even louder when he drove into her again and again while rubbing her little clit. Her eyes snapped open as if she could barely take a breath.

"Oh God," she cried. "Oh . . . that's . . . I'm . . . I'm going to . . ." Suddenly, her back arched and she couldn't make a sound. Her climax was so powerful that she remained that way until the pulsing orgasm had swept all the way through her body. He liked watching her as she trembled, and he enjoyed feeling her even more as she writhed slowly against him to feel him moving inside her.

When she was finally able to catch her breath, Eliza looked up at him. As Slocum crawled on top of her, she scooted back so she wasn't about to fall off the bed. He settled in and reached down to feel between her legs. She was wetter than ever and jolted at the slightest touch of his hand against her pussy. Slocum didn't say a word as he undressed her and then stripped off his own clothes so they were both completely naked.

Her skin felt smooth as silk in every spot that her body rubbed against his. For the next minute or two, Slocum and Eliza savored being so close, tasting each other's lips and feeling each other's bodies any way they could.

"I want you inside me again," she whispered while reaching down to feel him. Her fingers wrapped around his thick pole and stroked it slowly up and down. Slocum closed his eyes, savoring the way her hand worked him before placing his cock where she wanted it to be. As soon as he felt his tip brush against the wet lips of her pussy, he pushed his hips forward to plunge inside her.

This time, Slocum's entire body ached for only one thing, and he gave in to that desire by pumping into her like a piston. She was more than wet enough to accommodate him and she spread her legs open wide so he could thrust as deeply as he wanted. Slocum grabbed one of her hands and held it tightly as his other hand eased along the side of her body until he could cup the tight curve of her buttocks. Every one of his muscles strained with the effort of maintaining that rhythm, and soon Eliza was moaning again.

Slocum grunted as he felt his climax swiftly approaching. Grabbing on to her ass with both hands, he pulled her in close while burying his cock deeply between her legs. He let out a moan, emptying himself inside her as Eliza cried out and gripped him tightly.

Spent and exhausted, both of them lay there for a few minutes until Slocum gathered up enough strength to roll onto his side and lie next to her.

Eliza got up and left the bedroom without saying a word or putting on a stitch of clothing. She returned with a cup of water, which she sipped before handing it over to Slocum. "So," she said, "did you really catch the Beast of Fall Pass, or did you just say all that to impress me?"

"Did it impress you?" he asked before taking a drink of the water.

"A bit."

"Well, if that impressed you, just wait until you see what I've got in store after I've gotten some wind back in my sails."

She giggled and climbed on top of him. Her hands busied themselves by rubbing his chest as her hips ground slowly against his lower body. "I wonder if I can do anything to help with those sails."

"I can think of one thing."

Smiling, she eased herself down so her face was poised above his hips. She opened her mouth, wrapped her lips around his member, and started gently sucking.

"I think we're in for a long night," Slocum said.

19

Ed Taylor had come to Bennsonn as a vagrant. He'd scraped together enough money to pay for a ticket on the stage heading north from a trading post near the California border with every intention of trying his luck panning for Canadian gold. Having sold most of what he'd owned to pay for food and a new coat, he didn't have enough left over to get any farther than Bennsonn. The driver had left him off, recommending the mill as a good place to look for work. Mr. Womack saved his life by giving Ed a job.

Despite all his good intentions, Ed was first and foremost a drunk. Liquor was soaked so deeply into his body that he barely even felt much of anything when he indulged anymore. The warmth whiskey gave him helped to thaw out his innards on cold nights, but he drank whatever he could because it was the only thing to put an end to the shakes that had claimed him in the last couple of years. On the night of Slocum's return into town, Ed left the mill after sweeping the entire place for an extra bit of pay. Sobriety was an ache that bit all the way down to his core.

It was close to midnight and perhaps a bit past it when he walked out of the mill and locked the door behind him. The

152

air was crisp with a dampness that foretold an upcoming rain. More than anything, he wanted a drink of whiskey, and as he started the short walk back into town, he pondered each saloon in turn, weighing his odds of getting a line of credit large enough to put a splash of liquor into his chilled body.

"Wait a minute!" he said as he stopped dead in his tracks. Mr. Womack kept a small bottle in his desk for the occasional nip. Ed had seen his boss take it out every now and then to celebrate a profitable season or toast some bit of good news. Remembering it now brought a smile to his face. Surely Womack wouldn't know if there was just a little less of the liquor in his bottle the next time he reached for it. "He won't notice at all," Ed muttered to himself as he turned around and hurried back to the mill.

Every step he took brought a new pain as his muscles tensed and his joints stiffened like hinges that hadn't been oiled once during a long winter. Ignoring the pain as he ignored so many other things, Ed set his sights on the dark shape at the end of the road that loomed just out of his reach. The mill was a familiar sight to him and he'd walked to and from it so many times that he could do so with his eyes closed. Every bump in the ground along the way was familiar to him. Every creaking branch was something he'd heard at least a dozen times before. The stench that hit his nose, on the other hand, was new.

"Damn dogs," he grumbled while stuffing his hands deep into the pockets of his threadbare jacket. "Bringing more of them dead squirrels and leavin' 'em where they won't be found for—"

Those would be the last words Ed would ever say. The rest of that final sentence was cut short when he turned toward a large, dark shape he'd spotted out of the corner of his eye. That shape stayed low to the ground and moved like a puddle of smoky ink with a stench that was almost too putrid to bear. He squinted into the darkness, trying to make sense out of what he was seeing, but couldn't.

When the shape pounced on him with teeth and claws bared, Ed tried to defend himself. His efforts didn't amount to a hill of beans and only made the thing from the shadows work to pin him down for an extra couple of seconds. Once the thing was crouched on Ed's chest, the struggle was over. From then on, it ripped into him as if it were digging a hole in the ground and Ed's chest was in the way. It stuffed its short snout into the gaping, bloody cavity and pulled out whatever meat it could find.

When it had sated its gnawing hunger, the beast clamped its teeth around Ed's shoulder and dragged him away. Some small pieces of him were left behind. Some of the pieces weren't so small.

It was early the following morning when the Beasley brothers arrived at the mill. For once, Merle was in as rough shape as Darryl since they'd both spent the night drinking away a good portion of the pay they'd gotten from the sheriff for dragging the wild man in from the woods. The only thing that could have gotten them to drag themselves so far away from the beds of the soiled doves they'd chosen during the night's revelry was the promise of even more money from the man who'd put the hunting party together in the first place.

"Why the hell did we walk up here?" Darryl grunted.

"Because we probably would've fallen off our horses," Merle replied.

"I ain't drunk no more."

"Me neither, but my head's still spinnin', and if that isn't enough to put me on my ass, the fire in my damn skull is enough to make me throw myself onto a rock and hope I die."

Darryl laughed and immediately regretted it. Placing one hand flat against his eyes, he winced and staggered down the road that led from town to the mill. After tripping on a wagon rut, he stumbled a few more steps and eventually righted himself. "We almost there?"

Merle slapped his brother's arm. "You see that?"

"No, but I smell it. One of us still reeks of that idiot hermit's skins. I can't believe any lady would have us, whether we paid her or not."

"No, damn it! Look!"

As much as it pained him to do so, Darryl peeled his eyes open. Immediately upon seeing what was strewn on the ground farther up the road, he forgot about the throbbing pain behind his eyes. "What in the hell?"

"Looks like an animal carcass," Merle said.

"If that's a leg . . . it's too big to belong to an animal."

Merle drew the pistol from his holster as he ran to get a closer look. Wincing as the smell of dead flesh hit him, he said, "There's shreds of clothes scattered about. That means this definitely ain't no dead animal."

"That smell," Darryl said warily. "Did another killer get his hands on them skins?"

That question still hung in the air between the brothers when something exploded from the trees near the side of the road. Merle fired a quick shot at the thing that rushed at him and didn't know if he'd hit it or not before he was knocked off his feet. More shots were fired as Darryl rushed to help his brother. The thing that had attacked them leapt back and forth from one man to another. Both pistols had been silenced since the hands holding them were no longer able to pull a trigger. One of those hands wasn't even attached to an arm any longer.

20

When Slocum arrived at the mill, just a bit late for his normal workday, he once again found all the other workers gathering inside the main building. He'd already checked in with the sheriff, only to get a much colder reception than he'd been expecting. The lawman had handed over the payment for following through on the hunt and wouldn't answer any other questions on the matter.

"Go have a word with Womack," was all Krueger would say.

Rather than press the sheriff for any more, Slocum headed to the mill.

The crowd gathered in the main building was even larger than when Womack had delivered his last speech regarding the beast. After shouldering his way closer to the front of the group, Slocum could see that several of the men gathered there wore stars pinned to their shirts or jackets. One of those lawmen stood beside Womack. He was the same height as the mill's boss and had a lean, wiry frame. Somewhere in his sixties, the lawman had sharp eyes and carried himself as though he were about to pounce. He was clean shaven and mostly bald except for a partial ring of silver hair that circled around the back of his head.

Upon spotting Slocum, Womack hurried over to meet him. "There you are, John. So glad you showed up before we got started."

"What's going on here?" Slocum asked. "Is this some kind of announcement about the killer we brought in?"

"In part." Draping an arm around Slocum's shoulders, Womack led him toward the door to his office.

Slocum shook free and stopped before the office door could be opened. "Just tell me what's going on!"

"I'd rather do it in private."

"Why?"

"Because," Womack said in a voice that was almost too quiet for Slocum to hear, "more men were killed last night, and it looks like it was the beast's work."

Before Slocum could ask for details, one of the younger lawmen near the front of the group began to talk. Mostly, he was calling for silence from the others, but workers were already filled with questions, which they flung toward the front of the room. Rather than dividing his attention by listening to the answers given by the lawman, Slocum put his back to all of them.

Leading Womack away from the group without going into the man's office, Slocum asked, "Did that hermit we brought in escape from the cell he was tossed into?"

"No," Womack replied. "Sheriff Krueger or one of his deputies has been keeping their eyes on him every second since he was brought in."

"Then what the hell happened?"

Womack was shaking his head as if he couldn't believe his own words before they left his mouth. "Ed Taylor was found on the road outside. Or it's supposed to be Ed Taylor."

"Ed's the one who stayed after the mill closed to do odd jobs and clean up?"

"That's him. His body . . . parts of it anyway . . . were found on the road and in the woods. He was found by Merle and Darryl Beasley."

"Did they go after the killer?" Slocum asked.

Slowly, Womack shook his head. "Both of them were attacked as well. Darryl is with Doc Reece. He was torn up pretty bad."

"What about Merle?"

"He didn't make it."

"Jesus," Slocum sighed. "He's dead?"

"Afraid so. There were tracks near the bodies. Marshal Hackett is telling everyone this same thing right now."

"Then give me the shorter version."

"Whatever got to those men," Womack said, "wasn't the same as what got to Edgar and Dave. The tracks were animal tracks. Big ones."

"I want to have a look."

"I can't ask you to go back after that thing, John. The marshal will be pulling together a group of men to track it down."

Slocum's laugh sounded more like he was clearing something from the back of his throat. "Those lazy slugs wouldn't do anything until someone got ripped to shreds within town limits. If they would have gotten off their asses before, some good men would be alive and well today."

"Be that as it may, there's not a lot else to be done now."

"I want to go back out and hunt that thing."

Womack smiled and pat Slocum's shoulder. "I was hoping you might see it that way. When you three first came back, Merle told me that Abner Woodley was nowhere to be found."

"That's right. The crazy man said something about him, but I wouldn't put much stock in it."

"Abner was a fine tracker and he was always somewhat single-minded when it came to that beast. He was even working on a specially designed trap that was meant to hobble a creature of its size."

"Anything like a bear trap?" Slocum asked.

"I imagine so."

"Yeah, well, I know he caught a deer or two, but don't know about much else. Still, if he's out there tracking that killer, he may know a thing or two that we don't. All I'd have to do is track Abner and he might be able to take me the rest of the way."

Smiling like a cat with bird feathers in its teeth, Womack said, "I was thinking along those same lines. In fact, fortune has smiled upon us today, and I've found someone who earns his living tracking men. He's in my office right now."

"All right. Let's have a word with him," Slocum said. "But if I don't like what I hear, I'm riding out on my own. We don't have any time to waste."

"I agree wholeheartedly."

The lawmen were still talking to the group of workers taking up most of the main room. Although Slocum wasn't paying attention to any specifics, he could tell the marshal was spouting a predictable line of bull about how sorry he was about the men that were hurt and killed and how desperately he wanted to see that the good people of Bennsonn were protected. Thinking about the apathy he'd seen before and the fact that the marshal didn't even care to come out of his office after the first bodies were found, Slocum had to choke back the urge to shout a few choice words at the lawmen. When the door to Womack's office was opened and he got a look at who was inside, Slocum's instinct had nothing to do with talking.

"What the hell is he doing here?" Slocum barked as his hand reflexively went to the Remington holstered at his side.

Wincing at the sudden outburst, Womack shoved himself into the office while pulling his door shut before any attention was drawn from the workers or lawmen nearby.

Buck Oberman wasn't quite as surprised as Slocum, but he also reached for his pistol.

Space was limited within the office, but Womack managed to squeeze between the two other men in there with him. "Hold it, you two! Don't you recognize each other?"

Slocum stood with his hand upon the grip of his pistol, watching Buck like a hawk. Neither man had cleared leather just yet, but that could change in a fraction of a second.

"You're damn right I recognize him," Slocum said. "He's the man that's been trying to mount my head on his wall."

Buck was quick to respond, "That's only because you killed a good man and U.S. marshal out in Montana."

"What?" Womack said. Glancing over to Buck, he sputtered, "And . . . *what?*"

"That's right," Buck said. "My father was killed and all he did was see to his duties as a marshal. That bastard right there is the one who did it."

Slocum shook his head. "That isn't true and you know it. Max Oberman was killed by Deke Saunders when those marshals were riding after Deke's gang. I was there!"

"I know you were there. Deke told me all about what happened and how you gunned down my father so the surviving members of that gang could get away."

"Why would I do that?"

"Because you took a bribe," Buck said. "That's why."

"Jesus Christ." Looking to Womack, Slocum asked, "Why would you throw in with someone like this?"

"Because he told me he was a friend of yours!" Womack's face was red, and a layer of sweat had formed on his brow. Turning to Buck, he said, "You told me you were a friend of his."

"He lied just to find me," Slocum said. "Because he ain't nothing but a scheming bounty hunter and that's what bounty hunters do."

Buck shrugged his shoulders and grinned. "I did what I needed to do to find the man who killed my father."

"You know damn well I didn't kill Max Oberman."

"Then why did you run?"

"Because you were out for my blood and wouldn't listen to reason," Slocum explained. "I tried explaining myself to you once, but you wouldn't have it. Everyone else on that posse knew I wasn't to blame for what happened. I was even acquitted by a judge, but that still wasn't good enough for you!"

"Is that why you tried to hide in this little place out in the middle of nowhere?" Buck scoffed.

"I don't need this grief," Slocum said to Womack. "Darryl and Merle Beasley may have been loudmouth idiots a good portion of the time, but I owe it to them to put this whole Beast of Fall Pass matter to rest. You wanna take a shot at me?" he added while stabbing a finger at Buck, "then come along and take your damn shot when we're in the woods. If you feel like doing something that won't tarnish your family name, you'll help me put an end to this killing before you fire on an innocent man."

"Look," Womack said. "You two obviously have your differences, but good men are dead because of this beast. If you could put those things aside long enough, I believe you can get this job done a whole lot faster than if we left it to those men out there who are still doing nothing but spreading a whole lot of hot air."

None of the men in the office said anything as they sized each other up. In that time, the echoes of voices from the main room proved that Womack was right about all the talking going on out there.

Slocum kept his hand upon his holstered pistol, but still did not draw. Pointing at Buck, he said, "I did my best to keep Marshal Oberman from getting hurt. I agreed to do a job here and that's what I aim to do. I haven't run from any man or beast. If you want to help me, that's fine. If you want to face me like a man and force me to defend myself, that's fine, too. I'm done with you, Buck. I'm also done with you," Slocum added while turning to Womack. "After I collect my pay for this job, you won't be seeing me around here anymore."

Womack nodded. "I understand. And . . . thank you for seeing this through."

"Don't thank me. Allowing those blowhards out there to stomp after that killer would only make me feel responsible for them getting ripped to pieces." Slocum stormed out of the office and slammed the door shut behind him. Although the man giving the speech outside paused at the distraction, his droning voice quickly picked up where it had left off.

"Are you truly interested in helping us find the beast?" Womack asked.

Buck approached him. "Of course. All that other business about—"

"If this wasn't a pressing matter of town safety, I would've had one of my biggest men toss you out on your ear for spouting lies to my face," Womack snarled.

Buck nodded. "I understand. So . . . John Slocum. What is he to you?"

"He's a good man who's already put his neck on the line to do right by this town." Once that was said, Womack drew a breath and looked at his wall as if he could see through it to what was taking place beyond. "Tell me. What happened in Montana?"

"Slocum signed on to ride with a bunch of men my father had pulled together."

"Your father was a U.S. marshal?"

"That's right. They went out after a gang led by a known robber and killer named Deke Saunders. That bunch was hiding out after making a run that started in the Dakotas and was bound for California. Deke and his gang were cornered, so the marshals rode to clean them out. Things went to hell and my father was one of many who wound up dead. Deke Saunders made it through with a few flesh wounds. When the law brought him in, he was telling anyone who would listen that he knew the marshals were coming. He said there was someone working with the marshals who tipped him off."

"That was John?"

Buck nodded. "That's what Deke said and he was in a position where lying wouldn't help him much one way or another."

"Could be he just wanted to hurt Slocum."

"I went to ask Slocum about it a few times and there were words exchanged. When I went to find him again, he'd cleared out of town. I make it my business to track men, so that's what I did. Every time I nearly caught up with Slocum, I found bodies in his wake and a whole lot of folks who had some mighty bad things to say about him."

"Did anyone speak up on his behalf?" Womack asked.

"Sure they did. I figured I'd get everything straight after I caught up to him so I could look him in the eyes. Needless to say . . ."

"The more he ran," Womack sighed, "the guiltier he looked."

"If I've learned something while hunting bounties, it's that innocent men don't run."

"Depends on who's chasing them."

Straightening his hat upon his head, Buck walked past him and reached for the door.

"Do me a favor," Womack said as he made a point to stand in the way of the door being opened.

"You're the man paying me. Ask whatever favor you like and I'll let you know if it's within the price we agreed on."

"I don't know everything about what happened, but it sounds like this business between you and Slocum could be just some kind of misunderstanding. Don't do anything you might regret before you're absolutely sure you're justified."

"That's your favor?"

"Well . . . yes," Womack said.

"All right, then. Step aside so I can get to work."

There was no way for Womack to know whether or not his words had had any effect on Buck. He did know that the damage from him and Slocum crossing paths had already been done and blocking a doorway wasn't going to change a thing. So Womack stepped aside.

When Buck opened the door to leave, the marshal was still giving his speech in the main room.

Once he was alone in his office again, Womack snarled, "Damn it," and slammed his door shut.

21

Doc Reece did most of his work in a little house wedged between a dentist's office and a bookkeeper. Slocum went in to have a word with Darryl and was escorted to a small bedroom by an elderly woman who had a smile that shone from her heart. She had something pleasant to say, but Slocum was too focused on the next room to pay much attention. He did, however, return her smile as the old woman left him alone with the wounded man.

"I heard about your brother," Slocum said.

Darryl's face was always hard-edged, but this time it seemed about to crack like a mask made from old clay. "Yeah," he said. His hand was bandaged and his leg was covered by a blanket. There was nothing under a good portion of that blanket, which meant a generous portion of that leg had been amputated.

"Looks like it got to you pretty bad also," Slocum said.

"I'll make it."

"I'm going back out after that killer."

Almost immediately, Darryl looked up at him and said, "It ain't no killer. Not like that one we caught. It ain't no man."

"Then what was it?"

"I . . . barely know. It moved so fast. When it hit Merle, it

164

brought him down like he was nothin'. When it hit me . . . all I recall is being tossed about. There was pain at first," Darryl said in a quiet, haunted voice. "Then I was cold and dizzy. Thought I was a goner for sure."

Slocum's instinct was to comfort the other man, but knew any gesture along those lines wouldn't be received very well. "I'm sure you did what you could."

Focusing on Slocum as though he'd just remembered he was there, Darryl said, "It smelled the same."

"The same as that crazy hermit we found in the woods?"

Darryl nodded. "The same but worse."

"What about the wheeze?"

Darryl's eyes wandered off again. "No," he said in a distant voice. "No wheeze. It was strong, healthy, and fast. So goddamn fast." His eyes clenched shut, and he turned his head away.

Slocum felt like he should say something. Perhaps some words to comfort Darryl the way he would comfort anyone in his spot. Having lost more friends and loved ones than he cared to think about, Slocum knew all too well that no words would make Darryl feel better. Not now and probably not for a long time to come.

Stepping out of the room, Slocum was greeted by the friendly old woman. "I'm sure he was glad to have a visitor," she said.

"Can I see his brother?" Slocum asked. "Is he still here?"

She took him away from the room and lowered her voice so it wouldn't carry back to Darryl's ears. "He's upstairs until the undertaker can get him for a proper burial."

"I don't need much. Just a moment to get a look at his wounds."

"All right. Come this way."

When Slocum emerged from the little house where Doc Reece saw his patients, Buck was waiting for him. Slocum stopped at the edge of the boardwalk, squared his shoulders to the bounty hunter, and allowed his hand to hang down within easy reach of his holster. "All right," he said. "You've tracked me down this far. Let's have it out now and get it over with."

Although Buck didn't reach for his gun, he didn't make any peacemaking gestures either. "I'm not here for that. At least . . . not right now. Mr. Womack hired me on to find this beast and that's what I intend on doing."

"Thanks, but no."

"I would think you'd take any help you could get."

"I'd appreciate some help," Slocum said. "Just not from someone who I think will put a bullet into me when it suits him."

"Then you'll have to look over your shoulder because I'll be coming along whether it's with you or a few yards behind."

Letting out a frustrated breath, Slocum stepped down from the boardwalk and stormed past Buck. Every one of his senses waited for a hint that the bounty hunter was making a move against him, but Buck stayed put. "Don't expect me to put everything behind us just because you've decided to be civilized now."

"I was just about to say the same thing, Slocum." Falling into step beside him, Buck asked, "You went in to have a word with those two hunters that were wounded?"

"That's right."

"What did they have to say?"

"There's only one left."

"That's right. Sorry to hear it."

As he spoke, Slocum seemed to be saying things out loud just to think them through rather than have a conversation with the man walking beside him. "It sounded like the thing that attacked them wasn't anything like what we found out at Fall Pass. There were some similarities, but this thing seemed a hell of a lot worse. Didn't get a good look at all of the wounds, but what I could see didn't look like the ones made on the others that were attacked."

"How were they different?" Buck asked.

"The wounds on those two in there were rougher. Shallower and messier around the edges. No way in hell they were put there by a blade. At least, not the blades that attacked the first two men."

"Everyone's been talking about an animal," Buck said. "That's what this sounds like to me."

"That's not exactly how I'd describe the first beast."

"How would you describe him?"

"Come on," Slocum said as he walked down the street. "I'll introduce you to him."

Slocum didn't have much to say to Sheriff Krueger when he stepped into his office. He was there to see the man that had been dragged in from the woods, and considering what had happened more recently, the sheriff was inclined to grant him an audience.

While taking them to the next room, Krueger said, "Believe it or not, someone recognized this fella."

"The beast?" Slocum asked. "How could anyone see much of anything beneath all that filth?"

"Someone claiming to be his cousin. Brought a photograph and everything. Not that it's gonna change much of anything, but his name is Mick Doubrey. The beast, not the cousin, that is."

The next room was less than half as big as the one where the sheriff and his deputies kept their desks and gun cabinets. Most of the space in there was sectioned off into three cages, one of which was barely large enough for a man to sit with his legs gathered up close to his chest. The wild man Slocum and the Beasleys had captured was in the small cage, grabbing on to the bars and trembling as if he was about to jump out of his own skin.

"So," Slocum said as he stepped forward. "You've got a name."

"And you've got a gun," the wild man said. "He's got a gun! Both of 'em do! They wanna shoot me!"

"Shut the hell up," Buck said. "We got our guns because these lawmen are gonna hang you anyway and probably don't give a damn whether we shoot you or not."

"You got that right," Krueger bellowed from the next room.

Grinning, Slocum said, "You're Mick Doubrey?"

The prisoner didn't respond, but there was a faint glimmer of recognition in his eyes.

"You wanna tell me why you killed those men?" Slocum asked.

"I had to eat," Doubrey replied.

"Good Lord," Buck growled as his hand came to rest upon his holstered pistol.

Slocum's eyes narrowed. "Did you make that weapon you were carrying?"

"Had to honor the beast or it would get me," Doubrey said in a shaky voice. "Had to feed it. Keep it happy."

After just a few words came from Doubrey's mouth, Slocum knew it would be folly to try and make sense of them. He wasn't quite ready to write off his visit to the sheriff's office as a complete loss, however. "Were you trying to be the beast?" Seeing that the crazy man had drifted into his own world, Slocum pounded his hand against the bars to rattle him back to the present. "Is that it? You wanted to be another Beast of Fall Pass?"

"No," Doubrey said with a hint of a smile beneath his unruly beard. "No, no no no no."

"Then why dress like it? Why kill like it?"

"So I could kill like me. So I could be the man my momma raised."

"He's a bloodthirsty animal," Buck said. "And he wanted to be able to spill as much blood as he wanted without having to answer for it. Ain't that right, you piece of trash?"

Despite what Buck was saying or the contempt with which he said it, Doubrey looked at him as if he'd found a kindred spirit. "That's right. You understand."

"Sorry that I do understand." Looking to Slocum, Buck added, "If he kills and makes it look like an animal did it, nobody will come after him. Men like me won't hunt him down."

"And if a group of hunters comes along," Doubrey said while glaring at Slocum, "he won't be ready for no man. I almost got you, bastard son of a bitch. Almost gutted you."

"I've had enough of this," Buck said. "We can't believe anything that comes out of his mouth anyhow." After saying that, Buck turned his back on the others and left the room.

Slocum didn't have to watch to know that the bounty hunter hadn't gone far.

"What about the skins?" Slocum asked.

"Oh, I skinned some of them folks all right," Doubrey wheezed through a wicked smile. "Skinned 'em, chopped 'em, fucked 'em, licked 'em!"

Having sat at more than his share of poker tables, Slocum knew when someone was posturing. Coming from anyone else, Doubrey's vulgar words would have seemed almost laughable. But from the mouth of a lunatic, the claims weren't just disturbing. It was entirely possible they were true.

Refusing to react the way the other man wanted, Slocum said, "You were out there for how long?"

"Sixty lifetimes, asshole!"

"Answer my question or I'll shoot you in a dozen different places that'll hurt you so badly you'll pray for death. I wager I can keep you alive for at least a day or two in that condition. Even if I'm half right, that should make for one hell of a show."

Unlike the string of obscenities spewed by Doubrey, Slocum's words were spoken as if they were gospel. They struck the prisoner with a sobering effect, wiping the filthy grin off his face entirely.

"My . . . my skins?" Doubrey asked.

Slocum removed the lethal edge from his voice as quickly as if he'd thrown a switch. "The skins you were wearing when we found you. Where did you get them?"

"I . . . killed one of them . . . one of them things."

"What thing? Was it the beast we were looking for?"

Doubrey nodded. "There used to be two of 'em. One was old. He was injured. Got hisself stuck in a trap. I found him and . . . and shot him in the face. Even wounded and me havin' a gun . . . that animal still damn near took my head off."

"What is it?"

"I . . ." Shaking his head, Doubrey ran his hand along the bars of his cage. "I think it's a devil. Or a demon. Maybe his angel wings were bitten off and his . . . his . . ."

Recognizing that Doubrey was slipping into his own world and not sure he could pull him back, Slocum leaned forward to stare at him as though he truly cared whether or not the savage lived or died. "How long were you out in those woods, Mick?"

Doubrey blinked and looked at Slocum earnestly. Perhaps hearing his more familiar name spoken in a civil tone was a welcome change. It was just as likely that whatever whispers he was hearing in his head had just chosen that moment to let up. Either way, he seemed to be focused on Slocum and relatively docile when he replied, "Years. I . . . don't know how many. There were some winters and . . . and some summers so . . . so it had to be years."

"And there were how many of those beasts out there with you?"

"Two. Then . . . then just the one."

"And you managed to stay alive. Was the other one frightened of you?"

Doubrey laughed once, which sounded more like a breathy hiccup. The laughter that followed shook his chest and shoulders without amounting to much apart from a grating string of wheezing grunts. "I'd never believe a monster like that would be afraid of any damn thing, and I'm the one that was rollin' around in the woods."

"So how did you keep away from the other one? It was the skins, wasn't it?"

When he let go of the bars, Doubrey staggered backward as if he was somehow falling toward the back wall of his cell. "It was . . . the stench. That's how I found the one that was hurt. That's how I found the old man in the traps."

"Old man? You mean the beast. The male?"

Doubrey's nod was barely there, but it could be seen. Much like the man who'd given it. "I'd walked all the way from a trading post in Canada. Thought I was gonna die. Knew it. Spoke to it. Then I smelled it."

Trying to keep up with the wild man's babbling was a strain on Slocum's ears as well as his head. With some effort, he was able to recognize when Doubrey shifted from one track to another. He tried to nudge him back in the direction he wanted him to go by asking, "You could smell the beast?"

"Anyone with a nose on their damn face could smell it. I thought I was smellin' the angel o' death. Maybe . . . maybe I was." With a blink, he suddenly looked like a regular person who'd simply fallen on bad days. "Them woods are close to warm houses and a town where I could slip in to get what I needed on occasion. There was warm spots to sleep and plenty o' water in that stream."

"You liked it there."

"I did. So did them beasts. I skinned the one I shot. Damn near keeled over from the stench. You think they're putrid on the outside? Heh. Try cuttin' one open and peeling them like a potato."

"I can imagine," Slocum said through a forced smile. He didn't like playing along with the madman, but it seemed to be gaining him some ground.

"I thought, maybe if I smelled like one of 'em, the other wouldn't come after me like it came after them others."

"What others?"

"The other folks that rode down Fall Pass," Doubrey said. "I found some of 'em when I was passing through. Horses were killed and torn up just as bad as the men that had been in the saddles. Hell . . . even the saddles were torn up. A wagon was upended sometime after . . . or was it before? Anyhow, it was pulled apart along with the team and folks on their way to . . . wherever they was goin'."

"That'd be the Coulsen family," Sheriff Krueger said from the doorway. "They were killed . . ."

Slocum motioned for the lawman to keep quiet. "So the skin kept you alive," he said, prodding Doubrey to keep talking in the right direction.

"Yeah," the killer replied. Soon the clarity in his eyes faded, and his beard shifted as his lips curled upward to bare an incomplete set of crooked brown teeth. "But it won't keep you alive, nor anyone else who finds themselves lookin' into that thing's eyes. You and them others took my skins away and tossed 'em into the water. Thought it was real funny, didn't you? Who's laughin' now, you son of a bitch?"

Perhaps sensing how close Slocum was to drawing his Remington, the sheriff stepped forward and grabbed his shoulder. "That's enough of that," Krueger said. "No more visitors."

"Where did you find the old man?" Slocum asked as he struggled to keep from being dragged from the cramped room. "The male beast that was wounded. The one you shot in the head. Where did you find it?"

"It ain't there no more, you dumb bastard!" Doubrey wailed. He would have said more, but a wheezing fit doubled him over.

"I'll find it and bring its head back to show you. Just bet me that I won't!"

Throwing himself at the bars, Doubrey said, "It'll kill you. *She'll* kill you!"

"The hell she will. I'll find that spot and show you. Tell me where it is!"

"You'll die," the wild man shouted. "Just go two miles west of Fall Pass and half that north. Be my guest, you damn fool! You'll die in them woods because you ain't got my skins to protect you. Rot in hell, bastard cocksucking whore!"

Doubrey's mind had completely derailed this time, and it would be a while before he could be much use to anyone. Slocum stopped struggling with the sheriff and allowed himself to be removed from the room, where he was then shoved toward the front door of the office.

"I knew I shouldn't have let you two in there," the lawman said. "Once he gets all riled up, he's impossible for a good hour or two."

"I appreciate your time, Sheriff."

Doubrey was still shouting in the next room. His voice was strained so much that his words were barely recognizable above the grating wheezes he spewed.

Buck stood across the street, leaning against a post outside a butcher's shop. When he reached into his pocket, he flipped open his jacket to show the gun he wore.

"You want to draw on me right here?" Slocum asked. "Go right ahead. I doubt anyone will do much of anything until after the smoke's cleared."

Moving his hands a bit slower, Buck reached into his pocket, pulled a dented cigarette case from where it had been stored, and opened it. "Care for one?" he asked.

Slocum waved him off and started walking down the street.

The bounty hunter fell into step beside him. "Did you accomplish anything back there, or did you just want to make life difficult for that sheriff and his deputies?"

"I learned plenty," Slocum said. "As far as giving those lawmen something to listen to for a while . . . that was icing on the cake."

"Figured as much. I thought things might go smoother once I was outside."

"Did you? Was that your big plan?"

"Not really," Buck said as he placed a cigarette between his lips and struck a match on another post as he passed it by. "But I was hoping that was the case after I left. Tracking you down hasn't been easy, Slocum. Along the way, I've had to deal with a lot of men talking tough and spouting off. Guess it gets under my skin after a while."

"Then you're in the wrong line of work."

"Yeah, well, I've been wound up pretty tight since I put my father into the ground."

Slocum stopped and wheeled around to face him. "I told you once and I'll only say it one more time. I didn't kill Max Oberman. The fact that you're taking the word of a known killer over mine is a damn insult."

"Wasn't just one man who pointed a finger at you. There were a few."

"Like who?"

"A few men on that posse," Buck replied. "As well as a few of the men who rode with Deke Saunders."

"When we were attacked, it was at the worst possible moment while trying to clean up the rest of that gang," Slocum said. "We were bottlenecked, flanked, and outgunned at the one spot in our ride when we were most vulnerable. The only way for that to happen was if someone told those shooters where we'd be and when to expect us. That could have been any one of those men you spoke to. I didn't have anything to gain from what happened."

"And why would they all lie to me?"

"Why else? Because they didn't want to hang!" Slocum shook his head and walked off. "This is why I left town. There's no talking to you. You been through enough already, and I don't want to kill you, but I will if you keep pushing this with me. Do what you've got to do. From now on, I forget about the past and deal with you the way I would with any other son of a bitch who takes a shot at me."

"What if it was your father who was gunned down?" Buck asked. "How far would you go to make certain the man who pulled the trigger got what was coming to him?"

"Pretty damn far, but only if I was certain I was after the right man."

After just a few more steps, Buck caught up to Slocum and said, "That's what I'm doing."

"I said my piece," Slocum grunted. "You'll hear it or you won't."

After a few seconds, Buck asked, "What did you get from that prisoner?"

"A good idea of where to find this beast and what to expect when we do."

"I still think finding that tracker, Abner Woodley, is a good place to start."

"So do I."

"I can help," Buck said. "I may not know this area or much about this beast, but I can track a man through damn near any kind of terrain. You give me a few things to go on and I can make short work of it."

Slocum stopped and studied the other man. "What if I could tell you where to pick up Abner's trail as well as which direction he was probably headed?"

"If I can't find him by the end of the day, I should be able to get awfully close."

"He may be hurt. Or dead."

"That makes my job even easier," Buck replied with a smirk.

Shaking his head in aggravation, Slocum continued to walk toward the stable where his horse was being kept. "This is why I don't care for bounty hunters. They're as ghoulish as they are cold-blooded."

"Is that why? I figured it might be due to the fact that you're wanted for more than a few hanging offenses yourself."

"There's that, too."

22

Slocum felt like he could make the ride out to Fall Pass in his sleep, so he took it at a full gallop. The only thing that he allowed himself to worry about along the way was whether or not Buck would try to put a bullet in his back. He didn't concern himself with the beast just yet. After everything he'd heard and seen, Slocum knew that if he was attacked by that thing, he wouldn't see it coming and probably wouldn't feel much when it hit.

They reached the spot where Slocum and the Beasley brothers had started their original hunt. He dismounted and quickly found the place where the bodies of Edgar Fuller and Dave Anderson had been discovered. Pointing to where some of the bushes alongside the trail had been stamped down, Slocum said, "Here's where Abner's trail should start. Have at it."

Buck climbed down from his saddle and slid his hat farther back upon his head to clear his field of vision. "You keep watch while I have a look."

"Gladly."

So far, Slocum hadn't parted with much as far as what he'd learned from what Doubrey told him. If Womack had offered Buck an amount of money that the bounty hunter wouldn't want to split, Slocum wasn't about to give him enough to complete the job on his own. Of course, there would come a time where Slocum would have to tell Buck something in order to move things along at an acceptable pace.

"Slocum! Come over here and bring the gear."

Having already unloaded the things they would need, Slocum hefted a saddlebag over one shoulder and carried his rifle into the woods. The horses were already tethered and seemed to be almost as familiar with Fall Pass as he was.

"What did you find?" Slocum asked.

"Whole lot of tracks. Some of them fresher than others. Looks like at least three men came through here not too long ago."

"That would have been me and the other two who brought in Doubrey."

"Then that means this set of tracks," Buck said while focusing his gaze on the ground a bit farther away from where he'd started, "most likely belongs to the man we're after. Makes sense since they were covered up pretty well."

Slocum approached the bounty hunter, but made sure not to trample on the ground that was under Buck's scrutiny. "They were covered?"

"Yep. They were made at the same time as these here, which fall under the fresher ones. I'm guessing the man we're after set down a false trail and those two you brought along fell for it hook, line, and sinker."

"How can you be sure about all of that?" Slocum asked.

"Because it's the sort of thing I would do."

"I guess I don't see why Abner would cover his tracks if he was hunting a wild animal."

Buck wiped a bit of sweat from his brow. "The man in that jail cell wasn't an animal. He might have followed Abner's tracks if he knew he was hunting him. Also, was there any sort of reward being offered for the capture of this beast?"

"You know damn well there is."

"Sounds like two good reasons for Abner to cover his tracks. Either protecting himself from a wild man or keeping someone from taking his prize away. Those tracks lead away from here, but they're mighty hard to follow. It could save a whole lot of time if you knew where he might be headed."

Slocum sighed. He knew he'd have to cooperate with Buck sooner or later if the two of them didn't kill each other first. Since he'd had his fill of this stretch of woods, Slocum said, "He was probably headed west for a mile or two."

"That's a good place to start. Let's get moving."

Buck picked his way through the woods at an impressive pace, which meant he was either one hell of a tracker or searching for the perfect spot to try and bury Slocum. Every step of the way, Slocum was ready to defend himself. Even after going over a mile and a half through the brush, Buck hardly lifted his nose from the ground. When he finally did stop for more than a second or two, Buck pulled up something that had been tucked away so well it seemed to have appeared from thin air.

"Well lookee here!" Buck said triumphantly. The burlap bag in his hand was covered in dirt and leaves. It was so bulky that the bottom portion of it was still partially covered by the earth.

Already dreading the answer he might get, Slocum asked, "Is that a body in there?"

"No. The sack's too heavy for a small body and too small for a heavy one." Buck reached inside and pulled out a mess of bent, rusted iron. When he held the contraption at a different angle, Slocum could see the twin set of jaws and interlocking teeth. "Looks like a trap. There's a whole bunch of them in here."

"Those would belong to Abner, all right. I was told he was dead-set on getting that beast and that he'd put together some traps to get the job done."

"He must have been taking them somewhere when . . . aw hell."

Crouching down low and surveying the woods around him, Slocum put a hand to his Remington and said, "What is it?"

"I think I found Abner." Buck inched forward a few paces and reached down into the undergrowth. This time, he uncovered an arm that was caked in blood. "I could use some help here," he grunted.

Still wary of a double cross, Slocum approached Buck to get a look at what had been found. Sure enough, from his new angle he could see the vague outline of a partial body hidden beneath layers of dirt and leaves. He winced at the stench of rotten meat that had been unleashed now that the body had been uncovered.

"What do you think?" Buck asked. "This him?"

It was a man and it was mostly in one piece. It had also been killed by the sharper claws forged by Mick Doubrey instead of the stronger ones that had planted the last crop of men into a graveyard outside Bennsonn.

"Honestly," Slocum replied, "I can't say for certain. I never laid eyes on Abner. This seems like it would be him, though."

"Well, the tracks I was following end here. We've got the traps and we've come this far. It's too bad we don't know anything else that could help us get the job done."

Feeling Buck's stare boring through him, Slocum grudgingly said, "A bit farther west and then a mile north. That's where Doubrey told me he found the first beast."

"That supposed to be where its den is?"

"I would think so. You heard him blathering," Slocum said. "It was like pulling teeth just to get as much as I did out of him. Asking for it all to make perfect sense is pushing it. Although he did tell me about how he killed one of those things. Even though it came from a crazy man, the story made sense. From what he said and from what I've seen, this beast is fast but it's flesh and bone. Slow it down enough and it can be finished off."

Buck hefted the bag of traps up onto his shoulder and said, "These right here will slow down anything that needs legs to walk."

"All right, then. Let's finish this."

Between Doubrey's stories, Slocum's familiarity with the woods, and Buck's skill as a tracker, they found the beast's den in relatively short order. It was a large hole in the ground wedged between two tall pines and mostly covered by bushes that had been shredded almost as much as the last hunting party.

From a distance, the hole looked to be large enough for a

wolf to use as a home. When Slocum got closer, he uncovered even more of it to reveal an opening that was twice as large as he'd first guessed. The beast's familiar stench was overpowering, and that, coupled with the pungent odor of dead meat, told him that he'd found the spot they'd been looking for. He ventured inside with rifle in hand, picking his way slowly forward until his eyes adjusted to the shadows within.

The cave was large enough for him to step inside while hunkered down. Bones were scattered on the floor among carcasses that still had meat on them. A bed of leaves and twigs lay in one corner. Having seen that, he walked back outside again.

"Is that the place?" Buck asked.

Keeping his weapon at the ready, Slocum replied, "Looks like it and I'd say it's still being used. There's some pretty fresh kills in there."

"And some fresh scat right here," Buck added. "Has all the markings of an animal's den if I've ever seen one, and I've seen plenty."

"Let's get started putting those traps out. This thing is supposed to be lightning fast so it could be back here at any moment." Slocum went to the burlap sack that had been found and removed one of the traps. Until he'd pulled one completely from the bag, he didn't realize why they were much different than any other trap of its kind. This one was actually two traps connected by a chain. One set of jaws was slightly larger than the other and had a modified spring mechanism.

There were four traps in the bag. Buck and Slocum placed them near the front of the cave and pounded stakes into the ground which were connected to the middle of each trap's chain. "Near as I can figure," Buck said as he pushed one set of iron jaws apart, "the larger trap is the same as any bear trap. These smaller ones connected to them, though," he added while opening that set and gently priming the spring, "are something else."

"What do you mean?"

"It seems it would take a bit more to set them off, is all. Why anyone would want that is beyond me, but I guess this Abner fellow had something in mind when he made them."

"All I know is these were made for the beast we're after," Slocum said. "It's not like we can ask Abner what's what."

Buck stood up and looked down at their handiwork. All four traps were placed so that anything larger than a coyote would have to cross at least one of them in order to get into the cave. They were staked to the ground and the third one had just been prepared. Buck walked over to the fourth as a stench wafted through the air.

Crouching and bringing his rifle to his shoulder, Slocum warned, "Don't move."

"That thing is closing in," Buck said. "I can smell it."

"And I can see it . . . I think."

Keeping his eyes on the trap near his feet, Buck worked as quickly as he dared without putting his fingers at risk. "Where?"

Slocum's voice dropped to a cautious whisper. "Behind you. Just . . . don't move."

Buck's shoulders tensed, and he slowly stretched his arms out to try and set the smaller set of jaws. His back was to the tree line, which meant that if the beast was there, the bounty hunter would have to cross the ground littered with traps to get away from it.

Although Slocum saw some bushes moving and heard some leaves rustling, he couldn't quite make out what was causing the disturbance. Instincts born into every animal that had walked or crawled told him the predator was closing in, but he kept from doing anything that might tip his hand.

"Slocum?" Buck called out in a low, steady voice.

"I don't have a shot yet."

"It's moving away from me."

Slocum blinked. In the time it took for his eyelids to fall and rise, the rustling in the bushes had stopped. "It's circling," he said.

Buck finished with the trap he'd been setting and reached for his gun.

Something to Slocum's left made just enough of a sound to catch his attention. By the time he'd turned to get a look at what it was, the beast was already on its way. All he saw was a thick, dark body rushing at him like a shadow that had been spit up from the bowels of hell. Claws slashed through the air, and narrowed eyes glinted with reflected sunlight.

Slocum fired a shot just to try and divert it, but the beast wasn't afraid of the weapon. It slashed at him with the same claws that had gutted countless men, and only Slocum's quick reflexes kept him from being next in line. He twisted the rifle around to block an incoming slash. Although he kept those claws from raking through his skin, the rifle was knocked from his hands to fly into the surrounding bushes.

Falling backward just to buy himself some space, Slocum drew his Remington with all the urgency he would use if he was facing another gunman in an empty street. As soon as he cleared leather, he fired. Slocum couldn't be certain where he'd hit the thing, but his aim had been good enough to cause it to yelp and bolt in another direction.

Slocum waited until he could hear where the thing had gone or see some bit of movement to let him know where to put his next bullet. When he did hear something, it came from two directions at once.

Branches rustled somewhere to his right.

Behind him, heavy steps pounded against the dirt.

As he turned to the right to see the dark brown shape of an animal pouncing at him, Slocum felt a tightening around his throat as his next breath became trapped in his lungs.

Slocum's ears filled with a hellish snarl accompanied by the clatter of metal slamming against metal.

He lost track of which way was up since the ground and sky were tilting crazily around him.

All of this confusion lasted for no more than a second or two, but it dragged on for damn near a lifetime.

Slocum's backside hit the ground, driving even more wind from his chest. The beast had sailed over his head to land in the clearing outside the mouth of its den. Twisting around, he found Buck behind him lying on his stomach with one arm still stretching toward him. It was only then that Slocum realized the bounty hunter had grabbed him by the back of the collar to pull him down as the beast had been about to lop his head off. To do so, Buck had charged through the traps he'd set. Along the way, one of the large sets of jaws had clamped around his left ankle.

The beast was definitely a cat of some kind. Possibly a strange breed of mountain lion or oversized wildcat. It touched down upon nimble paws, skidding in some loose leaves and setting off two of the remaining traps while roaring loudly and clawing at the ground. As soon as its eyes found the two men, it lunged at them. Thickly muscled legs easily pulled stakes from the ground and the chains connecting the pairs of traps rattled noisily. Saliva flowed from its mouth and it slashed with both front claws to bring down its next meal.

In that moment, Slocum was sure he was going to die. Somewhere within his racing thoughts was the hope that it wouldn't hurt too badly when he was eaten alive. His finger squeezed the Remington's trigger, sending round after round into the beast without slowing it down. When the trap at the other end of a chain flipped over behind the beast's leg, its jaws snapped shut to grab hold of the ground. It was the first time the beast didn't seem like deadly poetry in motion. Even though it was only tripped up for one step, Slocum was granted enough time to send his final bullet straight through the animal's head.

It took one last step, one heavy paw thumping against the ground as if trying to punish the dirt below its dying body, and shuddered. Expelling one long breath, the Beast of Fall Pass dropped onto its chest before crumpling into a heap.

Slocum remained still for several seconds, watching the animal over the smoking barrel of his gun. Not wanting to be caught defenseless if the hulking cat found a second wind, he replaced the spent bullets within the Remington's cylinder.

"I . . . think it's dead," Buck groaned.

"Doesn't hurt to be sure." Taking careful aim, Slocum burned two more holes through the beast's skull. "There!" he said. "That wasn't so bad after all."

"Easy for you . . . to say. You ain't the one . . . who stepped in a goddamn bear trap."

Slocum holstered the Remington and moved around to the

trap that was chewing into Buck's leg. He grabbed its iron jaws in both hands and started to pull them apart. "Might be better to leave this be," he said while straining against the cruel mechanism.

"Take it off or your head will get blown off next!"

"You could lose a whole lot of blood."

"And if we leave it where it is, it'll saw off my damn foot and I'll still lose that blood. Keep working!"

Slocum tried to separate the jaws as cleanly as possible by lifting them straight from the wounds they'd created instead of pulling and sawing the iron teeth within Buck's flesh. "You saved my life," Slocum said.

"Yeah. I know."

"Quite a change of heart."

"I . . . didn't truly believe what those deputies and gunmen said about who killed my father," Buck admitted.

"Then why track me down?"

"Because I had to be sure." Although Buck's voice was somewhat weaker, he was clinging to consciousness with more tenacity than the trap clinging to his leg. "There . . . were some men who set my father . . . up to be killed."

"Crooked deputies? Deke's boys?"

"I found the ones I was sure about. They're dead. Now . . . I'm sure about you. That's all that matters." When the iron teeth were finally lifted completely out, Buck's entire body went limp as if the pain had been the last string keeping him up.

"That better?" Slocum asked.

"Still hurts, but yeah. Much better."

"I'm going to wrap that leg and help you up so we can get to the horses. I'd bring them here, but the woods are too thick."

"I know," Buck said. "I walked through them, too, but I won't be able to walk back now."

"I can help so you won't have to put weight on that wounded leg."

Buck nodded. He was pale, but still hanging on and willing to do what he could to climb to his feet as Slocum lifted him off the ground. "I found all the men I was certain had a hand in my father's death," Buck explained as he struggled to stand. "You were the last one. I wanted to talk to you before . . . question you face-to-face so I could see your eyes when you defended yourself, but you'd already gone."

"I'd already answered those questions. Several times, in fact," Slocum said.

"I wasn't ready to listen then. Now . . . I can see you're not a man who would gun down a U.S. marshal."

"Depends on the marshal," Slocum said. "As for your father . . . no. I would've killed the bastards that gunned him down if they weren't already on their way to the gallows when I left."

"I owe you . . . an apology." Now that he was upright, Buck tried to support his weight on his other leg and grimaced in pain. "Damn it all to hell! I was afraid of that."

"Afraid of what?"

"Twisted my goddamn ankle when the other got caught in the goddamn trap! Hurts like a bastard."

Slocum leaned into the bounty hunter a bit more and grabbed Buck's arm tighter so he could lift some more of the man's weight off his feet.

"Sorry for all of this, John."

"You don't owe me an apology for any of it," Slocum replied. "I would have come out here whether you showed up or not, and I doubt anyone else would have had the speed or the sand to get me out of the way when that monster pounced. I'm much obliged."

"We're even," Buck said in a voice that was quickly fading.

Slocum grunted with the effort of setting Buck down. He tied his and Buck's bandannas together, wrapped them around Buck's leg, and cinched them tight. Then, he pulled the bounty hunter up again to bear as much of his weight as possible on his back.

"What are you doing?" Buck asked.

"What I said I'd do. Getting you to the horses. You can't walk, so I'm carrying you."

"Just . . . you don't . . ."

"Shut up already," Slocum growled as he began tromping through the woods dragging the bounty hunter along with him.

"We've got a lot of ground to cover. Once we get back to town . . . then we're even."

Slocum fell into a steady pace, which was interrupted by him knocking his foot against a log and nearly falling over. After steadying himself and moving on, he said, "On second thought . . . when we get back to town . . . we're each having a bottle of whiskey and you're buying them. *Then* we'll be even."

Watch for

SLOCUM AND THE KANSAS SLAUGHTER

421st novel in the exciting SLOCUM series
from Jove

Coming in March!